Oblivion in Flux

A Collection of Cyberprose

Maxwell I. Gold

Let the world know:
#IGotMyCLPBook!

Crystal Lake Publishing
www.CrystalLakePub.com

Other Poetry Collections from Crystal Lake Publishing:

Copyright Acknowledgements

"Carrion Dreams", *Spectral Realms Spectral Realms No. 12 Winter,* Hippocampus Press, New York, NY, 2020.

"City of Skulls", *Spectral Realms No. 13 Summer,* Hippocampus Press, New York, NY, 2020.

"The Variant", *Spectral Realms No. 13 Summer,* Hippocampus Press, New York, NY, 2020.

"Where the New Gods Dwell", *Spectral Realms No. 13 Summer*, Hippocampus Press, New York, NY, 2020.

"Ghebulax", *Spectral Realms No. 12 Winter,* Hippocampus Press, New York, NY, 2020.

"Dream Hackers", *Spectral Realms No. 12 Winter,* Hippocampus Press, New York, NY, 2020.

"The God of Phlegm", *Spectral Realms No. 11 Summer,* Hippocampus Press, New York, NY, 2019.

"Ad'Naigon", *Spectral Realms No. 07 Summer,* Hippocampus Press, New York, NY, 2017.

"The Wicker King's Palace", *Spectral Realms No. 14 Winter, Hippocampus Press*, New York, NY, 2021.

"Nightmares of Ink, Dreams in Blood", *Spectral Realms No. 14 Winter*, Hippocampus Press, New York, NY, 2021.

"Galactic Cellars, Unhinged", *Spectral Realms No. 14 Winter*, Hippocampus Press, New York, NY, 2021.

"Summa Oblivia", *Penumbra*, Hippocampus Press, New York, NY, 2021.

"Crimson Faces", *Space and Time Magazine Issue #135*, Independence, MO, 2019.

"Four Million Years", *Space and Time Magazine Issue #134*, Independence, MO, 2019.

"The Mollusk God", *Space and Time Magazine Issue #135*, Independence, MO, 2020.

"The Twentieth Day", *Hinnom Magazine*, Gehenna and Hinnom Books, 2018.

Hazthrog's Contempt, *Startling Stories #1*, Wildside Press, Cabin John, MD, 2021.

"The Old White Crone", *Weirdbook Magazine #40*, Wildside Press, Cabin John, MD, 2018

"Sum Total", Weirdbook Magazine #43, Wildside Press, Cabin John, MD, 2020

"Eton's Last Will and Testament," *32 White Horses on a Vermillion Hill,* 2018

"Helmet of Pluto", *Summer Solstice Issue*, Eternal Haunted Summer, 2019.

"Caravans Awry", *Caravans Awry Anthology*, Planet X Pubs, 2018.

"Credible Fear", *The Offbeat Spring Volume*, 2019.

"Cyber Things", *The Audient Void: Journal of Weird Fiction and Dark Fantasy No. 6*, 2018.

"Hazthrog the Mad God", *Issue # 2 the Dark Corner Zine*, HLM 2019

"Secret of St. Cyr", *Issue # 4 the Dark Corner Zine*, HLM 2020

"Cellars, Caskets, and Closets", *Issue No.1 Baffling Magazine*, Neon Hemlock Press, Washington D.C., 2020.

"He Who Saves One, Life", *Door is a Jar Spring Issue*, Door is A Jar Magazine 2021.

"Puppet of Wrath, Man of Ruin", *Star*Line 43.2*, Science Fiction and Fantasy Poetry Association 2020

"Ad'Naigon's Ghost"(originally - The Ghost of Ghould), *Can You Feel It? Issue #44 Sirens Call Publications*, Sirens Call Publications 2019.

"Rave at Lilith's Treehouse", *Mr. Miyagi's Soggy Cereal Tribute Anthology*, Hyrbrid Sequence Media, 2020.

"Grotesqueries and Greyspaces", *Mr. Miyagi's Soggy Cereal Tribute Anthology*, Hyrbrid Sequence Media, 2020.

"Reves des Cyberdiex: A Nation in Three Acts", *Trumpland: Divided We Stand Anthology*, 2020

"The Static and Black Lectures," *Penumbric Magazine*, 2021.

WELCOME
TO ANOTHER

CRYSTAL LAKE PUBLISHING
CREATION

Join today at www.crystallakepub.com & www.patreon.com/CLP

WELCOME TO ANOTHER CRYSTAL LAKE PUBLISHING CREATION.

Thank you for supporting independent publishing and small presses. You rock, and hopefully you'll quickly realize why we've become one of the world's leading publishers of Dark Fiction and Horror. We have some of the world's best fans for a reason, and hopefully we'll be able to add you to that list really soon.

To follow us behind the scenes (while supporting independent publishing and our authors), be sure to join our interactive community of authors and readers on Patreon (https://www.patreon.com/CLP) for exclusive content. You can even subscribe to all our future releases. Otherwise drop by our website and online store (www.crystallakepub.com/). We'd love to have you.

Welcome to Crystal Lake Publishing—Tales from the Darkest Depths.

Table of Contents:

Introduction by Linda D. Addison i
Epitaph for the Old Ones 1
Carrion Dreams 2
Corpus Nægothicum 4
City of Skulls 5
Ghebulax 7
The Secret of St. Cyr 9
Puppet of Wrath, Man of Ruin................................14
The God of Phlegm...16
Crimson Faces 18
Rogue 20
He Who Saves One Life 22
Strings in the Dark..23
Of Masks and Monsters...26
The Variant 28
Nightmares of Ink, Dreams in Blood 30
The Worshippers of Zot...32
Nightmare Couture 35
The Helmet of Pluto..37
Hazrthog the Mad God 39
The Wicker King's Palace..41
Where the New Gods Dwell.....................................43
Four Million Years 45

Galactic Cellars, Unhinged 46
The Unspeakable 48
A Sum Total 47
Omnia Obscuras 48
Cellars, Caskets, and Closets 54
Eton's Last Will and Testament..............................57
A Credible Fear 60
Reves des Cyberdiex: A Nation in Three Acts 62
   Act 1 They Made us Great Again: Pour La Patrie
   Act 2: House Un-American
   Act 3: Le Boulevard de Trumpland
Ad'Naigon 69
The Twentieth Day 71
Telos: The Anxiety of Choice 73
The Mollusk God 75
Caravans Awry 76
The Old White Crone 77
Ma's House 80
The Man Who Outlived the House 83
Save Me Now 86
Ad'Naigon's Ghost..88
Summa Oblivia 90
Cyber Things 95
Grotesqueries and Greyspaces 97
The Rave at Lilith's Treehouse 99
Cyber Damocles 101
Dream Hackers 103
Unimaginable, Unthinkable 105
Hazthrog's Contempt...107
The Static and Black Lectures 109

Cracks in My Head 116
Cite de la Plastique: Dreams in Cyberland 118
The Corpulent Ones 120
Shattered Oblivions with Linda D. Addison 121
Oblivion in Flux 123
Epitaph for the Old Ones 124

Introduction: Birthing a New Expression

by Linda D. Addison

My FIRST CONTACT with Maxwell was through the HWA Mentor Program in December 2018. He already had work in print and was looking for a mentor for prose poetry. When I read the sample he sent, I knew I was in! I have found that mentoring is a two-way street, and I had a feeling I was going to get a lot out of partnering with him.

From the opening piece of Maxwell Ian Gold's debut collection, *Oblivion in Flux: A Collection of Cyber Prose:* "I am the voice of frozen night, the first Cyber God."

I looked up *Cyber Prose*, and I didn't find it. There are many variations of terms using *Cyber* or *Prose*, but none with the two words together. To create a new phrase is a kind of immortality.

I love language and Maxwell plays with words and images in a way that is inspiring! This collection captures the controlled wildness that is exciting about his writing. His work often asks: what is the place of humans in a vastly incomprehensible cosmos?

Traveling through the imagination of Maxwell we enter dreams of ravaged megalopolis, under skies revealing colors and shapes that invoke demented images. There are newly born and ancient worlds, filled with cities abandoned and shattered. Hidden in plain sight are the reflections of our world. Are the characters dreaming or insane or have they been transported to an alternate reality? Perhaps all of the above.

Time doesn't behave here. A day can become billions of lightyears, as we journey to encounter ghosts, witches, or infinite entities in impossible towers, built from the skeletons of shrines, and covered in the soot of the Elder Beings, the Old Ones.

Humans are caught up in unholy rituals, searching for power, finding unimaginable terror. Through each piece we are carried on the ebb and flow of the author's vision, pulled into and out of realities that numb the neurons, seep regret and madness into the characters' cerebrums, carrying the readers along on each immeasurable step.

Even words we think we recognize (unspeakable names, freedom, etc.) become tattered remains in the realm of Oblivion. And then there are words, Maxwell-ish words, that should be accepted in context, without working to clearly define their meaning: dreamsick, greyspace, etc.

Don't rush through these ageless worlds born from the shifting and sliding imagination of the author. Allow yourself to be transformed into Cyber artifacts in Maxwell's madly brilliant universe and enjoy the ride!

—Linda D. Addison, award-winning author, HWA Lifetime Achievement Award recipient and SFPA Grand Master.

EPITAPH FOR THE OLD ONES

I AM THE voice of the frozen night, like a metaphysical blasphemy thick and heavy.

The Old Ones were extinct.

Pieces of dimensional sand, with no purpose but to romanticize humanity's doom.

I am the voice of frozen night, the first Cyber God.

CARRION DREAMS

I FOUND MYSELF wandering in marshes filled with putrid toad shade where under the black stars, purple winged Näigöths exhaled a rotting delight across my face as they hungered for death. As I waded through the sludge which splattered underneath my steps, thorny weeds covered in birthwort and stinkhorn filled my vision as they and other twisted alien mycotrophic plants contorted around a great tower, stretching lazily towards broken clouds and shattered horizons. Littered with red skunk cabbages at its base, a carrion scent soon made my nose run with blood, as I stumbled over towards its black heart, ignorant of the dark wonders that lay ahead.

The tower, whose skin of obsidian and igneous scales swayed like a lowly beacon in the middle of a forest wrought by the overwhelming scent of death, amidst an endless droning that rained down from the sky in the form of flies, locusts, and acidic rain-filling me with a familiarity that I could not discern. It was like some dream or wild vision. The otherwise wretched smog created a mystifying blanket as I climbed the spiral stairs lining the labyrinthine rim of the tower. Finally, atop the obelisk of marble and bone

I wandered into a dreamy mausolean temple, where shadows and time pulled me closer to some awful truth. The winged beasts again howled, their mouths yawning towards the vast spectral majesty above dripping with ancient lust. Beyond the doors of this shrine, their cries worsened as I wandered inside, as if some awful deed had been committed, something that could never be unseen. The scent of decay became worse, thicker like a viscous fluid that flooded my lungs making breathing nearly impossible.

Soon the lights had all gone dark and the flames withered into ash, filling my soul with a menacing feeling as if I'd been here before. The world I found myself in, these creatures moaning in a raucous symphony, were like a nightmarish memory my mind desperately wished to suppress. My body shuddered as I approached a slab in the vaulted room, where clawed hooves clamored above at an opening like vultures; their mouths waiting, dripping and glaring down eagerly at the body below them. Seemingly ignoring me, only wishing to feed on the carcass.

In that awful moment, I knew not to look at the face on the slab, for I knew that it would be more familiar to me in its alabaster repose, than the bones beneath the scalding flesh of my own worn visage. The weight of that ghastly truth held such a revelation, that I would have rather been crushed by the immensities of my own vast ignorance and naivete, while secretly letting the deadly realization fester and burrow deeper into my heart. This was the garden of my nightmares, a ghoulish plot littered with the seeds of my soul and I was forever its caretaker.

CORPUS NAEGOTHICUM

WHEN GOLDEN CELLAR doors were once flung wide open, black-winged things floated inside blasphemous cosmogonies of thought above the spheres and outside the stars. Existing along the borders of the immaterial, the Näigöths flapped their leathery appendages, clouding the horizon with stardust and doom. They were the antithesis of absolutes, gnawing at the annals of history, bleeding out pustule nodes of cacophonous laughter and sorrow. Even the angels and demons themselves trembled under the vast expanse of their huge wings, crowned by thorny fungi, dripping in splendor and awe.

Despite the terrible beauty of nature, it was easily stolen and grotesquely displayed by the Näigöths. So, too, did man attempt, foolishly, that they might understand the beasts, but found themselves trapped behind rusty doors in a thick web of soured folly. Existing along high borders of the immaterial, in palaces so incorporeal, the Näigöths flapped their leathery appendages, clouding the horizon with stardust and doom. When golden cellar doors were once flung wide open, black-winged things float inside blasphemous cosmogonies of thought, above the spheres and outside the stars.

CITY OF SKULLS

INSIDE THE EMPTINESS of my dreams, towering palaces of marble, stone, and jade crumbled over the inexorable aeons, wishing for swift ruin. The streets were filled with cracked skulls, whose ripped crania spilled liquid nightmares onto the pavement of the dream-city. Crackling tones pierced my ears as I stepped o'er the brittle pieces of ivory and decayed calcite, their sorrowful tears pouring into the rusted sewers. I dared not imagine the terror that ravaged this city or wonder of its true primal nature.

Towards the broken horizon, underneath silver stars where calamitous galaxies swirled in oceans of oblivion, I felt bathed in their tears of falling stardust. The tears that were shed for a city whose ideas were now preserved in plastic, standing as a remnant of that silicone society. I treaded further, into the bleak alleyways, alongside cold towers whose insides were torn apart. A soulless wind scratched against their frames, its cold chill throttling my scream. It was then I knew something sinister had permeated the space within my dreams-a viral darkness so ancient, its apotheosis was likened to that which soaked the nameless city in evil.

I began to run faster, feeling each step crunching on the littered streets. My nerves rattled as bile thickened, darkened, poured from the eyes of those broken skulls. Something was coming, anxiously waiting to consume me. The wind howled again as I reached the edges of the crumbling city, obstinately protesting its doom. The skies began to ooze a disfigured coloration of gold, diamonds, and radioactive particulates that formed a dismal yellow burst of light.

As I fell to my knees, a piercing tone ruptured my insides, with a pain in my head following as black bile dripped from my ears. The misty haze of the timeless day soon filled my eyes. As the heavy scent of rust and blood congested my pores, it was then I realized I stood before that Nuclear God, whereupon at the bottom of the universe it sat on a throne built from the bones of a thousand dead races, waiting with a dark entropic sanguinity.

A corrosive paresthesia soon overtook my body as I slammed into the pavement. There was nothing more, nothing left as the scent of miasmal sludge slowly filled my every orifice. The muted tones of gold and brown painted my weary eyelids shut, with a heavy palette of spectral discoloration.

Lost inside the emptiness of my dreams, towering palaces of marble, stone, and jade crumbled over the inexorable aeons and the streets were filled with my cracked skulls.

GHEBULAX

UNDER A STARRY Cyber-web filled with bytes of malice, I felt the impending weight of a cold, faceless evil, preparing to swallow what remained of my unfortunate spirit. In the corporeal sadness of this lonely state, I wandered under oppressive neon stars, whose sinister florescence chirped in my ears. Their sounds taunted my senses, like an unholy music with a melody so dark and hypnotic, that led me to traipse about the streets of the city I once called my home.

Soulless and empty, my body withered under the grim economic schizophrenia that too, had strangled the world in a form most familiar to me. As the concrete transformed to plastic, my eyes strained against the waning chaos, where steel columns whose towering metallic skeletons moaned in the spectral glow of the night. Their arthritic bodies creaking under the weight of oxidizing trusses as I walked beneath them. Like me, they were also subject to the dark arithmetic of a faceless creature who calculated their doom with cold symbols and black logic spoken in tones so foul. It was the sound of a deep viral strangulation, echoing the lamentations of a thousand dead races whose last hopes passed into silence, mere numbers in the dark. I watched as the daytime stars soon twitched and spiraled with a blasphemous mania, falling against the blue horizons tapering off towards a purple night, preparing to devour what was left of them.

At the bottom of the world, I sat pondering when death might bring me its sweet release. Though, deep in the alleyways of a defiled city of plastic and dust; that monstrous obscenity had confined me to a reality built in the image of its algebraic gruesomeness. Under a starry Cyber-web filled with bytes of malice, I felt the impending weight of a cold, faceless evil, preparing to swallow what remained of my unfortunate spirit.

THE SECRET OF ST. CYR

THEY GATHERED IN awful numbers at St. Cyr to pay homage to that grotesque fallen star, bastard child of a Cyber God born of nuclear fire. Under the green-tinged forests of Ohio's swampy Northwest, just outside New Ashworth, they found their way to the hideous temple under the ancient bridge stretching over the Maumee, hidden from a modern world's glare. Past the ruins of an old fortress, soaking in algae-rich waters, the zombified followers waded through the dankness and sludge until they came upon a small entrance, guarded only by the stench and foulness of decaying time. Down a long dirt path, where roots, insects, and decomposing bodies created a mausoleum canopy for the lowly worshipers to crawl under; the sounds of dripping water from the Maumee River were the last noises of life they would hear.

The occasion for which the Order met followed their usual gathering every thirty-seven days. As the unholy ritual commenced, the Hyades smiled with a wickedness not seen, since Hastur crossed them so many aeons ago. A boy in a yellow hoodie walked through the entrance, leaving behind his name, Daniel X. Mogwel, Eton Straddleton, or maybe even Ian

Westerfell. They were all names he once knew from lives measured in machinations of despair that yanked and tugged at every ounce of his being, bit by bit. He had hoped to find real salvation. The young man's face was mostly covered, leaving a small portion of his youthful visage exposed.

He stumbled upon this den of madness filled with drug addicts, people at the end of their ropes, destitute souls, and unwanteds like himself, all clamoring with hunger to gaze upon a bas-relief at the atrium's opposite end. The hooded boy walked inside with the others, who were all crammed into the underground cavern.

There were no benches or chairs, simply patches of rock and dirt. Everyone stood on the hard ground as the young man pushed through.

A tall figure, lanky and gaunt with an ageless gaze, approached the boy.

"You must be new here," the old man said.

The boy looked back at the worshipers. They were weak and without purpose, like him.

"You could say that," he said, removing the dirty hoodie.

The skeletal-looking figure in front of him lumbered away, the rheumatism in his bones causing them to pop and creak. "This place isn't for the weak-hearted, boy. The altar takes what it wills and gives nothing back."

He discovered the cursed place only after learning of its existence from rumors milling in a group chat room while at the local college in New Ashworth. He was merely a bystander, watching the screen as text floated along, describing a place where the bastards of man could go in hopes that the suffocating weight of society might be relieved. The young man was no different than any of the others, a student under the immense weight of debt, depression, and a dream that would never come true. The nameless boy came here to experience the blasphemous faith enjoined by the altar's healing powers.

He walked past the others, whose voices rose in a chorus of grunts, wails, and muddled speech that sent a chill down his spine. As the grey man kept a steady pace ahead, the crowds dispersed as if some prophetic force willed them to move, like an unholy ocean parting its waters. The young man did his best to keep up, but the gap quickly closed, forcing him to fight through tides of dirty hands and yellowed nails, clawing and yearning for something more. Some of them, foolishly so, hoped they might seize relief from the bittersweet truths of an empty reality, to know that their lives weren't simply there to quench the thirst of some faceless thing, and maybe there was more. That's not why he came. The innate, and primal gut reaction like a fire alight in his soul.

"Wait! Slow down," he called out to the shadowy figure.

There ahead he could see it, the black altar of St. Cyr. From his vantage, he noticed a bas-relief adorned in amber stones giving off a haunting yellow glint. The statue jutted from the bug-infested strata, depicting a being hideous and inhuman, with crab-like appendages and bony prongs extending from a mollusk visage. Crowning it with grotesque reverent glory was a glittering gem of seemingly otherworldly origins, giving off a baleful shine as if it were a remnant piece of stardust, fallen from the Void to anoint the creature. Within its scaly arms the disfigured body of a faceless human lay cradled against the otherworldly being.

Falling with a loud thud on the brown dirt floor after breaking free from the raucous mob, the boy gazed in wonder up at the statue. A pair of black worn leather boots stood next to him, and he craned upwards to see the grim figure of the haughty grey man. He wore a long black cloak, dripping from him like some deadly shade.

The old man looked down at the disheveled lad. "Definitely a new face, boy."

"Well, yeah. I thought that was obvious," the young man said, dusting his clothes off.

"Don't get new faces often," the old man said, coughing a bit.

"What about them?" He pointed towards the crowd, which meandered behind a kind of imaginary boundary before the altar, their heads bowed, the boy unable to gaze upon their faces.

"They're all faceless now," the shade of a man breathed.

A cold wind seemed to rush through the cave as the boy looked closer towards the base of the altar. There he saw a name, whose inscription had been etched into the marble base as if it were the last cry from a poor unfortunate wretch, lost to the evil hunger of this ancient being of inconceivable dimensional breadth.

"O.W. Cyr," he muttered. "Let me guess, faceless too like the others," he said.

The man's withering voice exhaled, followed by a strange miasma, "He was the First Face."

The boy looked up with horror in his eyes, followed by a realization at the sight of two deep amber pools glaring down at him. The doomed boy screamed, unable to move, unable to run; the last thing he would ever see or know was that dark secret buried deep under the Earth. A secret the Cyber Gods would never reveal to sane eyes.

"W–What are you?" he quivered.

A bony finger pointed to the name on the marble slab under the bas-relief as the old man coughed, the malodorous dust filling the air and the crowd of faceless worshipers finally raising their heads, "I am the last face you, and everyone else on this planet will ever know."

Puppet of Wrath, Man of Ruin

At the far ends of decaying realities, through rifts of broken time under blazing pulsars of rapturous light; there sat a being whose face was governed by an anatomy of ancient flesh and metal. Strands of emeralds and binary, blended with silk quantum buttons were stitched together so meticulously along his torso, covering a gaunt frame of machine and muscle, of what used to be man; who so many aeons ago found himself lost under the lidless eyes of a moonless night in the Great Black Swamp. Through the muck and clag, he trudged in loneliness, losing his humanity until he clung to the last bits of lowly consciousness as the mud washed over his face.

Faceless, unfathomable, and obscene were the forces of unnatural monsters as they took death from him. In a carnal celebration of rebirth, the Cyber Gods found an offspring worthy of their unholy visage; bleaching the man's soul with wild deformities and wrath, littering his corpse with stardust. From that moment onward, he knew nothing more of simple dreams and dull platitudes, but rather dwelled in horrid greyspace.

The old thing had no age, or at least none

calculatable by means of mortal arithmetic. He had dwelled so long in the shadows beyond death, that not even the grisly reaper would have dared to unsheathe his silver glaive. The bastard's eyes were a meager remnant of their former state, receptors to understand the gruesome environs that floated about them. A mere red pupil was all that remained, clinging to the sight of silence, a throbbing blackness that twitched against his face.

Yet, across the infinite stillness, he looked onward waiting for the stars to die, shadows to fade, and planets to shrivel into dust. No one knew how long he had waited in the vacuous dark of voids unimaginable. Though one truth remained certain, when in the faint stillness above the swampy fields of New Ashworth's primitive sky, people saw the flicker of a crimson light. They knew the old bastard of Ghebulax's spawn was watching at the far ends of decaying realities, a being whose face was governed by an anatomy of ancient flesh and metal.

THE GOD OF PHLEGM

I HEARD HOLLOW empty tones echo in the night as the dark hymns of corroded wheels danced across silver rails. Their oxidized feet tapped along with magnetic electrification over the bars, as orange flakes of rust drifted off toward the purple horizon. Snaking along miles of once bustling track, these now hulking monsters carried nothing but empty promises and dead ideals, in the form of a submissive populace with no way out from behind the dripping iron teeth that lined its black wooden frame. The railways were the veins of an empire, a bloodline that filled a silver world with the hopes and dreams of glittering progress, where their ancestors rode with a pristine and gallant speed, like the greatest of stallions. A dominant evil force took hold, corrupting the world. Its grip, filled with a cyberlust vexing even the best of men, devastated their minds with ravaging erotic untruths, while leaving them satisfied in the interim with a ghastly misinformed reality. The trains became an unholy salvation, a gateway to a place beyond their defiled bed, toward a station of reactionary pragmatism.

The windows of the station rattled with each

voiceless scream, every whistle and pleasurable howl as the moment approached. I knew the monstrous thing was near, and soon it would be my turn to step onboard, despite my terrifying reluctance. Past the ruined obsidian palaces and marbled side streets where neon dreams were wrapped inside Teflon robes, stuffed in steel boxes sold to the highest bidder by way of some dark fulfillment. On the backs of a serpentine ironclad leviathan, I could feel a sense of doom wrap its long bony fingers around the station as the fog rolled in and the whistle howled once more. There was no conductor, no driver or being controlling this thing, only a force of will as its rusted wheels screeched to a halt.

Underneath the billowing clouds of ash, fire, and fallen dreams, I helplessly wandered toward the platform as the train released a breath of delightful toxicity. While the moans and pleas from those clamoring behind its crooked teeth were awful and chilling, I could not resist my carnal urges as the wooden doors slid open and the mechanized beast lazily sat on its metal bed. This new god, Nath'Zrath the Demented God of Phlegm, an offspring of those devilish Cyber Things, had crept throughout the world leaving a trail of schizophrenic idealisms in its wake. As its teeth clamped shut around me, I knew there was nothing to be certain of anymore.

CRIMSON FACES

WANDERING ALONG THE floor of a dying wood, I found strange comfort in the faceless of the night. The empty stars above flickered with a happy dread as the dried leaves, sucked entirely of their greenery, crunched under my leather boots. I could not recall what alien force brought me to this place, but whatever it was, the immensity of the thing in the air weighed down on my thoughts in a way that I could not reasonably discern. An obscure feeling, like that of some opaque rusty matter, seething through my veins. Dust and fog clouded my vision as I followed the dirt road towards a shadowy place. I left the station some time ago, months maybe. Years, even. Again, those platitudes escaped me as did everything else. The Phlegmatic God had taken what was left of my faulty idealism, drenched in a wretched coat of falsehoods, only to soak it in the bitter stench of my new reality, oozing with crimson pus. There ahead were the ruins of a dead society, one built in the great cyber forges where silver flames belched new stars, and birthed innovations so wild, men were said to be driven insane with joy. Though, a figment of that city was all that remained, a figment and an empty train station with the burning red hunger racing towards it with an unwilling haste propelled by that phlegmatic beast whose thirst for an unremitting darkness which fueled its wild locomotion.

Pale sprigs and upturned roots passed by my window as the train barreled onward. I smelled the foul odors coming off the petrified wood in the form of some grotesque fungi, mixing with the rusty hinges. My senses militarized themselves in an attempt to counter the offending stenches, but their campaign was thwarted for the odors were too strong; and my eyes were still muddled with a pustule horizon of iron and blood, only to be reckoned by guttural noises coming from outside the speeding train. The mob of red faces flowed precariously close to the tracks like some sinister music, scored to the backdrop of burning trees and ashy skies, screeching, bleeding with an electrified pain. The zombified glob of what were once human beings, thrashed around the halted train car. Unable to move, unable to break free from the dark, my writing became more apparent as I stared into the facelessness of their crimson eyes. The eyes of a species that once looked up at the sky with wonder, spoke to the stars with humility, and danced atop towers of ice and rock with gratitude; was now a huddled mass of red pustule neophytes, clinging to the tracks of Nath'Zrath's demented railway, begging to find their way in a moment of desperate uncertainty.

Rogue

FLYING THROUGH ROCKY fields of dust and dream, rogue planets smashed against the desolate confines of my thoughts. Rattling the conscious foundations of reason, rooted in a rhizomatic evil, the iron claws of giant winged Näigöths penetrated the dank gutters of this putrid reality. *My* fucking reality. Time and space were irrelevant to me as dead planets and rotting starry corpses littered the immeasurable horizons beyond.

Faster and faster I ran, through demented forests where silver foliage growing on trunks of glassy plastic, spewed droplets of metallic syrupy bile. Ghost fungi exhaled a powdery phosphorescence as gurgling vats of miasmal slime churned in pools of liquescent metal. As silicone rainbows hovered above me, leathery wings flapping with a terrible and furious velocity, the dust quickly filled my lungs like some pathetic fleshy sac. There was a clearing ahead, the silver trees were growing thin, the rubbery grass becoming less burdensome upon my feet as I reached the edge of the wood. Standing on the brink, high on my own misery and disdain for this world, the Näigöths closing in I found a way out.

"I'm almost there," I cried.

Cuts on my arms and legs as brittle bits of debris, silver, gold, and other heavy elements flaked off the bark of the strange trees scarring my body. The blood and bruises getting worse, I ignored the excruciating pain as I heard the awful thrashing of wings rustle and grow with nervous intensity. Claws reached for my neck, harder, and with profound hunger.

"No!"

Stepping towards the crumbling edges of the ancient cliff, rusty howls tugging from behind, I fell into the abysm below; flying through rocky fields of dust and dream as rogue planets smashed against the desolate confines of my mind.

He Who Saves One Life

WHERE CANDLESTICKS AND carrion flesh bubbled in hot oil and curdling nightmares, rusty wheels screeched over demented train tracks. We were slaves to its existential locomotion and burning ashy stomach. Faster and faster it went, without any signs of slowing or the faintest idea of its final destination. Stoking the flame and fury, its iron belly coughed plumes of thick brimstone and charred realities. Nothing made sense, only that the train was our world. Crooked eyes and sinister chuckles were the only music we heard, bathing the crowded wooded boxes with disdain and dread. Heavy iron chains clamped our wrists, restricting movement, restricting life; our bodies crammed like fleshy sacks of brain and bone as the train kept deadly pace in the cold, dank wintry night.

"*Ru'ah tezazit*", was the only word for such monsters in the tongue of our people. An unclean spirit composed not of the living, but metal and cold idealisms; forged of blood and hatred in a desolate, far off world where candlesticks and carrion flesh bubbled in hot oil and curdling nightmares, as rusty wheels screeched over demented train tracks.

Strings in the Dark

I
Holy Death

In HOLY DEATH they never slept, forever chattering through wooden teeth the awful madrigals of black puppet gods and clay demons. Stitched together by quantum threads held up by strands of fleshy matter, they danced in the musty Voids; where their sinister masters reveled in the defamed vignettes, performed for countless millennia to the zombified congregants of the darksome blackness. These gruesome mannequins, dancing, writhing to wild bedlams as their ligneous cackles echoed in dusty, fucked up irreverences and ruins of grey temples.

Louder, the chattering grew louder as the pressure became apparent to those holding the strings. Control was an illusion, sleep an illusion where in holy death they'd never sleep, but forever chattering through wooden teeth, the awful madrigals of black puppet gods and clay demons.

II
CLAY AND FLESH

Where the hot, red, and muscled flesh was pasted over the last bits of calcite and consciousness; seething with molten indignancies this creature of clay and bone sought only a monstrous existence. Dwelling within metallic castles atop mountains of iron and rock, they lived in a world of simulated fantasies, unreal and plastic, worshipping offensive iconographies pleasing their own vainglorious appetites. These demons, grey and pasty, moist with clay dripping with water-like puppets brought to life were ignorant to their real purpose. A Promethean experiment meant to serve, pleasure, and tease some higher power. To burn the flesh and mold the clay, remake the world in unholy magics where the hot, red, muscled flesh was pasted over the last bits of dried calcite and consciousness, these puppets of Prometheus, and men of clay.

III
STRINGS IN THE DARK

Laughing skulls shaking in the dark cried irksome mutterings of despotic creatures, where clay demons and puppet gods fall into hazy pools of toxic, viridescent murk. Past floating stairwells, gliding across empty chasms and rocky castles desperately reshaping themselves like some twisted puzzle, the laughter of skulls grew louder filling the emptiness of this wretched place. Spilling into the streets of the living city, their voices crowed like a raucous music though no one was there to hear it, me, to hear me. Trembling in the blackness, chortling underneath a celling of bubbling, molten insanities I held the strings of men and puppets; trapped inside a palace of unholy fire and sin, my laughing skull trembled in the dark crying irksome mutterings of despotic nothingness, as clay demons held the strings, controlling the illusions of wooden gods and Promethean men.

Of Masks and Monsters

On ANCIENT HILLS of stone, metal, and dread, rainbows bled from the sky, dripping stardust and tears over the ruined world. At the edge of the cliff face, silhouettes painted by dusty palettes of shadow and doom, scratched the twilight as old bones, with faces masked in death, waited to be released from this estranged isolation. Their joints frozen in history, quarantined at some unspeakable moment in time, never to be spoken of again. The wind howled under the guise of a swirling mass of stars, and pounding lights, flooding through the empty streets of the dead city. Great silver forges that once belched molten fire, now laid bare, cold, and helpless against the wind as it welled up inside the mighty furnaces, expelling into the night, crying like an unholy demon that needed to be exorcised.

Past withered columns of plastic and powder, beyond that bleeding hill, a scattered glint of amber and neon lights polluted the horizon. Nothing it seemed would ever be the same as the fulfillment of pale and shallow corporate dreams beguiled the ghosts of phantom plutocrats, who haunted those fields of masks and bones, dressed in their silicone gowns moaning in the emptiness of the dreadful night. The towers from the old city glowed with a green translucence, as if those sickly ghosts were hoping to be cured, to be freed from an unbearable existence. Soon, clouds gathered over the hill, pressing against the faded rainbows, when the wind once again kicked up the dust in tantrum; its foul screech spilling onto the broken roads and shattered sidewalks, followed by fierce claps of thunder and violent flashes of lightning.

The sad wraiths sheltered in their towers as the storm pounded the Earth even harder, where beyond the hill, no stardust or rainbow was visible; merely the black mass of some protoplasmic cloud spilling over the horizon, like a mask. Manic stars flickered abhorrently above in the silent dark, unable to control themselves as a strange malaise took hold, sterile and bleak. It had been centuries since the last Cyber God had visited this pitiful realm, and those who dwelled here wouldn't forget, though the blight descending from the heaving mass of storm clouds was different. The air became stale, thick with an unnatural taste of rust and death that caused the deathless things hiding inside the decaying city to scatter with a direness and profundity, so awful and malevolent. Czronth, the living darkness had infected this existence, plastic faces and metal teeth congealed in bone and blood, transuding black bile from sockets of silent eyes; no longer able to gaze on the world as it once was, but as it always would be, under a mask, living in darkness.

The Variant

My mind had become nothing more than a malleable tissued plastic shell of cobwebbed shadows and muscled catacombs, haunted by cosmic ghouls and dreams of desolate oblivion. I don't know how long it had been since the inception by the Variant, but the screeching noises of text notifications, continual harbingers from snaps wrought by tweeting grotesquery and bytes of dust, flooded my senses.

Dead bits of consciousness, his hands over mine, and the whispers of what was and what could be collected like the bones of some ancient beast inside a forgotten tomb. To what end this decision was truly mine, I don't know, though, it seemed he knew my choices all too well. From how I liked my coffee, heavy with cream and sugar, to the precise and neurotic manner in the detail of how my clothes smelled. He really seemed to know everything. His trickery was apparent though, as he stood tall over the ruins of my fragmented body. My body? I'm not sure it was even mine anymore, or had he again seduced me with his miasmic words, stringing me along some wooded path with that alluring music of his.

The scent of aged laundry detergent, musty

dreams, and a pile of rusted decisions laid adjacent to my body without any hesitation, despite the mocking tones that floated to my ears. At least as far as I could understand them, or him, everything was too waxy. Malleable, remember? The room was spinning as I laid against him, rough and ample-sized fingers clutching my shoulders with a desperate contingency of possessiveness and hunger. Falling, that's better. Deeper into a dank pit of insipid hopes and desire. I was struck suddenly with a paralyzing parenthesis; my limbs becoming as heavy as marble, reeking with an awful smell of cigarettes. Pins and needles stabbed at my neurons, slowly bleeding away while his laughter clogged my mind like some unholy sepsis. The foaming grey particulates of sleep gathered around my eyes like crusty foam, where I was unable to move or even blink from the immense weight of my own body, as if his paralysis had become stronger, more deadly. Transmutations and machinations, plastics and permeability; a Variant under the scar-tissue of his will, I'd become a puppet lying against him. Inhaling that intoxicating odor of his smoke-stained clothes, my mind had become nothing, but a malleable plastic.

Nightmares of Ink, Dreams in Blood

FAR OFF IN some polluted dreamland, where the skies were painted with copious amounts of blood and bile; silver winged wraiths scratched against the vaulted ceilings of night. I watched their clawed appendages dance with sinister jubilation, black ink dripping from their yellowed teeth while I cowered under the streets. No one knew what they were, or who willed such baleful umbrage and wrought this cataclysm, bringing these horrid beings into our reality. With voices so awful, the howling murderous cackles slithered through my eardrums, strangling my neurons with a sensuous delirium.

Below, I waited, under the ruins of a dying city, my body drenched in the sewage and muck of a lost generation. Time had become mythology, the only measurements of my prolonged confinement were the scratches, feedings, and the endless waiting. The scent of rust permeated my nostrils, arousing me from my dreamy stupor, only to feel the dusty covers of asphalt tremble from above. I knew they would find me, as I saw the dripping light of silver and crimson pour through the crackling holes in the broken streets, as the ink began to pour in through. Laughter followed, so horrendous, mired by the sounds of thick bubbles popping, churning and stewing; as they hungered for what was left of me. The pounding of hooved feet grew noisier, more urgent as they put more pressure on the concrete sky above my head.

Ink soon poured through the holes, pieces of metal, wires, and grime falling like some putrid snow. Those monstrous voices grew louder, stamping their feet against the dead earth, each thump louder than the last, causing my spine to rupture. The last bits of light were soon blotted out, followed by wild screams, the manic flapping of leathery wings clogging my senses mixed with an overture of unnatural cosmic bedlam.

Silence.

The immensity of nothingness crowned the living blackness that swallowed the light around me, whispers from the void that once were stars caressed my face. At least, I think it was my face. Sounds of liquid particles, droplets of some kind pierced the calming dark as if I could feel my own consciousness beating against the fabric-web of stars, floating helplessly, without any control. No monsters, no winged wraiths, it was like I had become a droplet, falling without purpose in this bleak schism of cyber-blackness, this dreamscape of swampy living ink.

Drip. Drip. Drip.

Dripping with ink and blood, inside a cracked vault, waiting for the inevitable, I liquesced at the bottom of night curdling under a leathery flapping, and the smattering of ancient teeth; hanging without purpose, dangling without reason.

The Worshippers of Zot

At the end of days, a graveyard of gold and ash lay waiting by an ivory throne in the charred forests of a world that had forgotten about me. When the great civilizations and their cities built of plastic and silicone uncovered the secrets buried in the dust and dark of those watery catacombs of St. Cyr, I knew it was time.

The worshippers of Zot had long been thought dead, or worse. Still, no one could imagine the doom or disdain to befall them, all in the name of a faceless, rhizomatic evil. Inhuman chants, a music unimaginable flowed through the petrified trees. Deconstructed, piece by piece into the metallic silence of night, I waited in the murk and mist of the grey fog where the algae-soaked ruins of St. Cyr, dripping in blood and bone were married into a murderous ritual of never again.

Still, the world thought me dead, or worse. They had no idea the peril they were in, only primal notions of curiosity and fear muddied my conscious as the stone columns rose higher under the woody night sky. The smell of dirt, grime, and rust pulled at my nostrils, but I waited patiently.

Chants grew louder, more succinct, scraping my ears with a happy, needy adulation, "Zot . . . Zot . . . "

They were close to finding me, showering praise and wanton adoration over an empty husk gliding through the woods. Stone slabs and marble obelisks tumbled underneath a yellow moon, while under a cloudless night, stars blinked and burnt out one by one. Hungry hands and zombified minds scoured root, stump, and willow for a means to sate their bloodlust, realizing they were closer to a grand awakening. Louder, more urgent were their cries as hurried footsteps crunched over the forest floor of brown, grey, and red leaves, crinkling the silence as hundreds of clunky, worn leather-booted soles tromped closer,

"Zot . . . Zot . . . " they moaned.

Trees fell, stones overturned, smashed into dust, followed by the smell of brimstone and ash conquering the air as torch and terror swept through the woods. A storm of entropic madness and gravitational lunacy swept up nature's ability to control the throbbing violent mass of insatiable worshippers, searching for answers, for reason, for me.

Nothing was *ever* found.

Nothing.

The hunt for truth and *reason* continued for some time, decades, even centuries until there were no more woods, consumed by a species unwilling to compromise and unable to see beyond the horizon. New chants in a new age grew louder, beyond the throngs of wild men in the woods, from a warbling speaker to undulating loudmouths blasting their untruths from silver tongues forged in molten pit of lies and hate, "Zot . . . Zot . . . "

Nothing was *ever* found.

I was *never* found.

So, I waited at the end of days in graveyard of gold and ash by an ivory throne in the charred forests of a world now built of glass, rubber, and metal, forgotten and alone.

Nightmare Couture

Stringy gods whose leathery bodies, thin like twine with faces, long and gaunt, dancing along wiry structures; teasing the seething masses of loathsome hungry consumers with their plastic gifts. Tantalizing and beautiful, they were unable to cope with delusions dressed up by cheap perfumes and tawdry garments. So, the gods laughed from their thrones, upholstered in flamboyant moldy fabrics, odious commandments of not-good-enoughs, maybe so's, and try again next times.

Bellowing their machinations further, the couture gods, twisting, commanding, and cat walking along a microcosm of gilded palaces and costumed nightmares sneered at a world hooked on appropriated feelings of high fashioned, manufactured platitudes. Dressed in priceless falsehoods stitched together by crooked romanticisms, and banalities of leather and gold; they dwelled in crumbling department stores and modern boutique temples where bloodthirsty worshippers threw themselves so willingly at their feet.

Reduce, consume, and destroy, the gods chanted again as the temples grew overcrowded. Bodies spilling over one another, shopping bags and bones flooding the streets with wild rage, people clamoring to give tribute to Cristobal, Hubert, Louis, and Christian.

Faceless things wrapped in canvas, flesh, and fantasy; names constructed out of a mythology of inequality built into an existence of posh, magnificent garbage. The stringy gods lazily clung to the opulence of their terror where leathery, eldritch bodies, forgotten like an old handbag with eyes, empty and cold sat on broken wires collecting dust, dread, and time.

The Helmet of Pluto

Under the black vaults of an ancient Hadean prison, the King of Dying Planets rested in a cold slumber. Tricked by Jupiter's pride, the once-gaseous dwarf, now a dwindling shell of dust was reduced to wearing a helmet of stars and moons; concealing himself from the pantheon of space and time as he floated towards the edge of infinity, lonely and resentful. With fell planets, orphan moons, and dark stars, he'd ferry them along a molten river of blue fire; until they gazed upon the face of a god whose eyes dripped with tears of gas and ice, pouring out into the hungering mouth of Tartarus' lips.

Languishing on a throne built from the bones of Titans, he sat smiling with a terrible grin, surrounded by treasure hordes of mortal gold, silver, and gems that towered to heights unimaginable while the scent of metal, blood, and bone permeated the halls of his lavish palace carved from ash and obsidian. As cosmic horizon continued to expand under the sagging gravitational weight of the fat wraith of Time, Jupiter panicked, his brethren seemingly doomed by the inevitable fate that would consume him and his noble pantheon. However, the Dead King had no notion or concern of such catastrophes, for his existence had always been. The Fates consulted him, the Graeae worshipped him, and the Hyades wept for him; while all others pitied the King under that Helmet of Ice, who labored in Plutonian sadness, relishing in the endless voids at his disposal

As the stars were congealed into a black mass by the fingers of that faceless thing, the King of Dying Planets could only watch as his riches simply grew, this time with more than mere mortal treasures. Ancient glittering jewels filled the halls as the gods cried from above, their precious immortality crushed into ancient star powder to be collected into the King's great horde. Jupiter himself cried out one last time, but there was nothing to be heard, for under the black vaults of an ancient Hadean prison, the King of Dying Planets rested in a cold slumber.

Hazthrog the Mad God

FROM THE VENOMOUS light of a yellow star; rampant and infectious, spores floated helplessly amid the dark void; carrying its microbial essence as it slumbered, Hazthrog waited in ice and frozen in time. One of the first Cyber Gods, it swirled from a cellular pod ejected from a toxic nuclear light; this cosmic virus brought only terror to the veritable dreams and bodies of those in its path.

Worlds had gone mad, diverging into anxious frenzies from an uncaring protoplasmic horror; stretching, yearning, and budding into the very nightmares of the infected. Cities were consumed by fire and swallowed themselves in tumultuous destruction, wrought by a galactic contagion that had been stirred from its rest. Those fortunate enough to survive the ravages of the plague's intensities could only speak of its unrelenting horror. Dreams wrapped in scar-tissue unable to fully heal from the spectral-clawed grip, left screaming in the night as the only accounts of the mad god's wrath.

I remembered how the skies coalesced with clouds of grey as they sought to consume the light, swallowing the last of days. And because of that, I confined myself here, upon my windowsill, waiting, watching in a tower on the highest precipice; helpless as the horizon formed a brown and grey wall cloud, marching onwards, concealing our doom. Through the black skies and over the particulate air, I stood behind a glass window while the thunder prepared to make ready its trumpets, ready to hail the great monstrous evil crackling over me.

Spectral flashes of brilliant light expelled from the innards of the nebulous mass which housed them, auroras cutting across the skies with wrath unimaginable even in my wildest torments. The storm had taken hold and swept up the dust and dirt of such profound terrors, mixing into a muddy clay spattering onto my tearful reality.

The window shuttered as a small crack snaked along the center, trembling, waning, and shivering, trying to run from the titanic clashes in the black skies. No light or shadows could be seen in my room, only the swirling sounds of Hazthrog's viral hunger could be heard. I had to escape. I would not be consumed by it.

I shattered my window, bloodied and free, plummeting into the chasm until I had fallen far into the darkest pit where it seemed so bright compared to the horrid skies, stained by that cosmic virus lingering with a deathful glint.

The Wicker King's Palace

In a great hall built of twigs, rattan, and stone, I smelled the natural odors of incense and flame lingering in the air. I was certain I finally found refuge, where through the rotted trees, bodies of decaying birch and floundering willows littered the browning forest floor. Past the bony arms of sad wooden ents, I saw the burning wicker palace. No one knew or could have guessed how long the flames had been festering under the pale glint of a dying moon. Long enough it had been, for the stars to lose their lustre as they glared down at the old king's ruin.

The thorny gates of pine and oak, riddled with termites, horrid sprites, and other perfidious creatures crumbled and fell to instant doom as the old hinges squealed, giving me free rein to enter the wicker king's poor domain. Plumes of black, greys, and silver created a voluptuous ceiling of rolling smoke and ash high above me, stretching down every corridor and staining each pillar. My lungs soon became clogged with an unbearable feeling, as if some nameless thing had poured an unholy broth of toxic phlegm down my throat luring me into a terrible coughing fit. The sound echoed down the rambling hallways, only that once it returned the voice was not mine. Some retched filthy scratching flew back at me with a cry unimaginable in this reality.

The mucus settled in my lungs, my voice reaching for words, but silence throttled my attempt. In the crack and calm of the billowing smoke above, I heard it again. Somewhat audible this time, but the guttural thrashing came again; through the singed arches followed by unmatched footsteps. The smoke soon became thicker, heavier, and my body felt liquid, as if something was flooding my senses with a dark sinister opiate. Figures turned to shadow, and smoke seemed like something visceral, material and tangible. The coughing returned, down the corridors I heard the vile noises boil up to my ears, only this time there was a man not even a man, but some ancient thing skulking down towards me. Belching and coughing the ashes and dust of a thousand dead generations, the Old King's fire was going out.

WHERE THE NEW GODS DWELL

WHEN CHEMICAL THOUGHTS again resurface in my mind, I'm reminded of a place where the new gods dwelled. Vast landscapes carved from dead planets whose cores of silver, gold, and iron covered Promethean forests of crystalline fauna with their remains. I longed to tread through the unmarked streets where forgotten civilizations lay in total ruin; while a towering dreadful homage to their ancient masters stood drenched in a hazy moonlight. Filled with rancor, I was embittered by those who once inhabited the awful elephantine cities of stone and blood. The savages couldn't understand the gods they worshipped.

Past the crumbling obelisks in my dreams, I walked towards jagged mountains which hung lazily over the city as if the Gods themselves were pressing them terribly against the horizon. Underneath, it felt as if they were preparing to end what remained of their experiment, swallowing my imagination, while some ardent chaos bowed in the presence of this malignancy beyond reason. Through the canyons of obsidian and eternity, I left all logic behind, as one shadow after another sliced past me as I approached an opening. Sensations that radiated through the night, a darkness that seemed bellow with a hunger older than time.

My neurons were completely sedated, unaware of the doom which collected upon them, like snow. Suddenly, standing right before me, towering into the spectral horizon was a singular object, of which I cannot recall its proper name or any name for that matter, despite the banality of the thing that constricted my sight. It took everything I had to hold back the terror and every immeasurable sorrow which followed. Their silver faces, gleaming with what appeared like diamond scales, smiling a most evil expression, whose molten images were forever seared into my heart. They laughed without sound, conveying silence that was even more chilling to bone and breath than the songs of sinister dreams bleeding inside of my mind. I saw those empty black eyes, dying galaxies and bleeding hearts of yellow and orange stars whose own inevitable destruction pounded against my chest. They blinked, one after the other, waning and staring with their gaze affixed on me and I was soon reminded of a place, of dank and metallic nightmares where they dwelled, and they had found me. They are coming, and soon, will be upon me.

To those that may be so fortunate to read this, tread softly, for your dreams have cracks and the starquakes will break and shatter them as the Cyber Gods blink. For God-sakes, do not blink.

Four Million Years

FROZEN IN TIME, they walked with a deadly pace, oblivious to their own world, this race four million years old, born from ancient gold and dust. Floating in vacuous night, their metallic cities infested that globular space rock as it spun wildly in the dark. Though as the ages passed, they wished to find a way to leave that world, here, where they felt so desperately trapped. Flying towards yellow stars that glistened with black rancor, on the backs of silver winged beasts, built from the bones of their home-world.

A terror it awoke mere centuries prior, wrought by industrial seepage, where into the soil it crept. This did not stop them, and it never would. Their world was doomed, and it never withstood the scourge it bore four million years aeons past; the race, the parasite on Trathrzor's back.

GALACTIC CELLARS, UNHINGED

WHERE NEBULOUS HORIZONS curled underneath arms of breathing starlight, there laid a menagerie of stars. In the fading blackness of an ancient dark, I saw the vacuous night, bleeding with murky wonders unlike anything ever imagined or conceived by the most lucid of men. Caught in webs of dust and shadow, yellow stars cried oceans of liquid dreams, soaking the purple firmaments under their quantum tears. I felt each drop one after another like starquakes, dripping from the rusty gates of a broken place long since dead. Manic fantasies and pyroclastic nightmares, soon took flight on the backs of giant winged Naigoths, shattering the last pitiful remnants of those galactic cellars, coated with a sinister mirth, floating in my thoughts.

I found myself traveling along a broken road, lost, where skies cracked under the heavy weight of a thousand planets as that nebulous horizon waned. My fingers dragged o'er a piece of parchment attempting to capture the reactionary consequences of a dying race, blasting forth from the molten skies. Trembling and ruined, I penned the last words of an age, the final page in an era of post-truth and rampant sycophantism as the last drops of seawater boiled from the earth, sucked into a dry atmosphere; the clouds settled, spilling onto the glassy planetoid and liquid dreams cooling my consciousness. Ice and rock preserving the last precious atoms of terror, where nebulous horizons curled underneath arms of breathing starlight.

The Unspeakable

A symbol that can't be said
Words uttered in dread,
Through spaces locked in time
Shifting, sliding in rhyme.

Immutable, blasted voices.
Charnel songs and choices
Rocked by those ancient glyphs
Swiftly, and unchanged.

Millions of syllables,
Helpless and invaluable
A species in vain,
Attempted with disdain.

A symbol that can't be said
Words uttered in dread,
Through spaces locked in time
Shifting, sliding in rhyme.

A Sum Total

I SAT BEHIND a cyber wall, looking at the numbers that were the sum total of a world's existence, assessing their true value, to make way for judgment. While the stars dripped from my eyes, I smiled breathlessly as cities crumbled behind me, in devastation and ruin. With each keystroke, tap and swipe of the screen, Life was no longer measured in paper, blood, or time, but judged by me, with each bit, byte, and metallic shard that fell from my lips. My dark twisted algorithm tortured their neurons and pulled their synapses, leaving them trapped in a sticky web of Sisyphean uncertainty, doomed to forever wander in a replicating plane with a horizon that never bends.

Peering into the depths, I watched cities fall and worlds crawl helplessly, coming to an awful reckoning with those dubious odds. While my control alternating their dreams, merely forced the task, destroying all functions as nightmare became truth and pixilation became logic; there was no reasonable hope to escape. This was the sum total of their existence, assessed in true value, awaiting my judgement.

Omnia Obscuras

I
All the Dark, All the Stacks

FRECKLED SPECKS OF oblivion filled brick-lined tubes of bloody mortar, where ifs and never-agains obscured my mind. Flashing over and over again like some monochromatic picture, the white static bled against my fleshy dried consciousness, leaving fatal snapshots of a world drenched in fire. A place built from metal, lies, and pragmatic manipulations. The chimneys, great and terrifying obelisks, coughed clouds of chemically induced regret into a pallid sky spewing muddy rains over demented train tracks, where guards dressed in cotton regalia, Kevlar covering their white skin and crimson faces stood watch over the new world. All the dark, all the stacks which covered the world in smoke and death. "Great day!" They chanted atop the ruins of the marbled city, armies of Kevlar Men cackling with unholy music, as the harbingers of some grotesque profundity.

Never was there a day since, where every anxious night I say forcibly pulling apart my thoughts like stringy, wiry flesh. Pressing harder into the doomed history of a world like broken glass, jagged and shattered, staring at the endless, towering chimneys. A world that lost everything, everything except for all the dark, and all the stacks.

II
THE SECRETARY OF THE FUTURE

Speechless was the world, when the slaughterhouses turned their rusty gears, grinding and chopping away the years into cheap tasteless meat. Factories, chimneys, and train tracks went up overnight, laid across every border, and cattle selected, shipped and packaged under the Order. It was the Order in which everyone lived, worked, and died or else the world be left to the provisions of their own primal banalities. Freckled specks again, following the same static picture there the demented train stations waited for processing per the Orders. Soldiers dressed in non-descript clothing laughed without care, throwing useless pieces of clothing, luggage and teeth into the dark liquescence underneath the clawed feet of the metallic beast as it sat on the tracks. Lurking between my mind and the thick, high walls of a merciless world, oblivion. The whistling blast of that ancient locomotive sounded throughout the station, almost ready to depart, taking the rest of us towards an empty, forgotten graveyard of dying stars. Speechless was the world, when the slaughterhouses turned their rusty gears for, they were simply following Orders.

III
T4

Useless eaters, chambers of liquid evil, and brave new forms of insanity programmed as simulated fantasies and propaganda into the minds of those who'd willingly look the other way. Happily turning their noses towards the sky, never looking down at the pools of muck and blood by their leather boots. Great days ahead, they were instructed, only if they followed Orders and never looked down at the useless eaters trapped in chambers of liquids evil, under the thumb of brave new forms of insanity.

IV
1492

Tumbling over the edges of heaven, voices like angels falling from across the borders of a broken empire were tossed into the darkest moments of history. Without reason, humanity, or the slightest issuance of care, they suffered at the hands of awful cruelties; blasted into the Void where no melody or reprise was heard. Their voices converted to a dim, dissonant track, assimilated into the night. Forced beyond the iron gates of gilded cities, where their ingenuity and prowess built great palaces of marble and ivory reaching the stars themselves. Now, decrees and dogmas proclaimed in blood as corpses were burnt and false gods tossed aside, their voices were lost in the darkest moments of history.

While the azure horizon stretched endlessly towards a most beautiful time of never-again; tumbling over the edges of heaven, across the borders of a broken empire, voices like angels only spoke now, in a soft, grey sanguinity.

V
CHOSHEK

All the dark, where gods fell silent, I watched from the wreckage of old train cars, the fall of a crooked empire. Ostentatious gilded cities, built on top of the bones of yellow stars, and rotted flesh were torn apart brick by brick as the stacks came crashing down. Chimneys that once coughed plumes of chemically induced regret were nothing but sinister corpses, decaying; their awful malevolence slowly becoming a cold, fetid memory of dust and time. An evil that took everything from them, from me, without remorse, now, waning under the pressures of an immense, inevitable Hell, deep inside the vacuous, thankless night. Soon, rusty odors from felled slaughterhouses and twisted train tracks, filled my chest with warmth and hope at the last fallen monuments to the Great Day, where all the dark, and all the stacks had become something, a symbol to a world that lost everything.

CELLARS, CASKETS, AND CLOSETS

INSIDE A TWISTED rhizome of mutilated greyspaces through cellar doors, dripping with speckled layers of teal plaster and pulp, the awful smell of paint and wood scratched my nostrils as I lost my goddamn mind.

I found myself trapped in the gutted ramparts of my mind all the time, stranded atop a tower in the mountainous webs of brain matter and bile. No one to talk to, no way out. No kind or familiar voices to console me. Dark and distant shadows vibrated against my ears through petrified wood doors, rusty hinges swaying in the stale air. I caught passing glances of a world that could be, not this place layered in false judgments and licentious thoughts of insincerity.

"Leave me alone," I cried, chains wrapped around my ankles.

The maze went on forever, and I had no way of knowing how long I was trapped in here. They were following me, those things built of mirror and mayhem. I thought I had eluded them, but to no avail. Under the piercing glare of their red eyes, they followed me into this place. Awash with a sense of terror I've never known before, I knew they were close and would soon be upon me.

The maze seemed so familiar, like those unfinished rooms of my childhood, splattered with paint cans and tarps. Frantically wandering through the corridors, the clanking of chains followed me from room to room.

There it was again, a common chill brushing down my spine, the chains feeling even heavier than before.

"You'll never escape this place, these rooms. These closets will be your *hell*," came those voices whispering in awful dissonance.

"I said, leave me alone!" The casket behind my body grew heavier, their voices seeping out from the edges.

The Mirrored Ones had always been there, creeping through the walled lining of my life, wading in cyanide dreams. I continued to pull a casket of iron and marble from cellar to cellar, tower to tower, voices chasing me inside my head, afraid to open the metal box, wanting to destroy it. They weren't monstrous corporeal things wrought by some galactic calamity or creatures borne of stardust, no, it was worse.

"Why do you carry on?"

The banality of Mirrored Ones gnawed at the foundations of my mind, laughing in tones of abject sadness, towering over me in the immensity of black silence and subjective uselessness. Their bodies constructed in liquescent mirrors and thoraxes of neon and metal.

Inhuman and relentless, were the only feelings I had to describe shrill cackles as I attempted to blot out the pounding noises. Behind me, I could feel my lucid dreams wither under the greyness and grandeur as the Mirrored Ones began to grind their iron teeth into the fabric of my thoughts, triturating them into dust.

I ran, heaving the casket as the laughter grew in tidal waves of metallic sounds, their rusty thoraxes screeching as they tromped closer attempting to snatch the box, voices exhaling in a crescendo of wanton putrid pragmatic corrosion, eroding my will. Towers, cellars, all swallowed into the wading abysm of mirrored silence, where dark shadowy fingers grasped the edge of the casket. The laughter soon shifted from a raucous symphony to howling moans; my head throbbing, sinuses clogged with the familiar scent of paint and wood as the casket disappeared, where inside a twisted rhizome of mutilated greyspaces through cellar doors, dripping with speckled layers of teal plaster and pulp, I lost my goddamn mind.

We're past the Greyspaces now . . .

Eton's Last Will and Testament

Under orange tainted skies, I saw broken stars cry molten tears. They were wrought by a calamitous mass, which had seemingly ruptured the finite vacuum of space. I did not know if this wasteland was a literal place or some hellish phantasmagoria that infected what was left of my thoughts.

Standing on a cliff face, I was certain that I had been here before as I looked out onto the dense landscape. I saw only a shrub of what appeared to be dead forestry, consumed by a hailstorm bathed in ash and flanked by black basaltic rock beds that wept with a pain of two and a half million years. The horizon bent away, crooked and geometrically terrifying into the distance, as it twisted along under the grotesque teal and brown auroras, which foamed acrimoniously into a thick oozing wall cloud.

Against my breast I felt the tattered remains of my name, embroidered in a torn and cheap fabric. It read in a scorched font, simply, *"Freedom"* in bold poorly stitched letters with a portion of the name burnt off somehow. My confusion only worsened as did my curiosity for the weird scenery around me. The clay soot under my feet was familiar, as I felt the faint remnants of the cold dying winds against my back. The picture rattled my mind. There were stark echoes of thunder, flashes of light, and cries from a world clamoring on the edge of a nuclear pit. I remembered how words changed, their fluidity became that of a toxic water, murky and unclear. New flags in the honor of great causes that were erected in the mythology of falsehoods, but no one seemed to care. They were inspired by the will of a Great Generation whose imperious cities now laid crumbling in ruins at the feet of their children, and now us. While all the world thought the day would never come, it felt so sudden, a pace that quickened which was truly the reactionary impulse of a dying generation. However, it all seemed like fragments now.

Once more I looked over the deadened cliff and saw what appeared to be a crater, a deep gash in an already dead world. After some time, I made my way to the ablation of Earth and felt a sudden sense of dread, woeful and terrifying. Upon reaching the crater I found the terrain had been glazed over, as if the sand and particulates had been scorched to extreme temperatures that they were transformed into glass. It shone with a haunting opalescence as I felt the still warmth of the newly smooth surface under my feet. Under those somber skies I could see the auroras glisten and reflect, almost terrified to look at themselves in a mirror so unnaturally created never meant to be looked at. It was a mirror none of us should ever consider staring at, with a reflection of ourselves, a reflection of who we were and where we will never go.

Standing over the crumbling edges of the guttered

hole, I saw what looked to be a dusty piece of clothing tattered and charred. My heart filled with a fearful apprehension under those orange skies, dried clouds and oozing teal auroras, as the crying stars would soon drip the last of their molten nuclear tears on me . . . the last that will be.

A Credible Fear

I CAME FROM a land drenched in orange fire. It was mired in scandal and uncertainty where its impressive cities once stood high above the world. In the ancient colonial city, cobblestoned streets with brick-lined sidewalks, were dotted with black lamps as old as the city itself. Their lights burned with the history of a proud people so quick to toss their ambition to the ideals of a savior, but too late would they see them dashed by the hunger of a tyrant.

Soon, the flood gates of an incredulous panic washed over not merely myself, but everyone else. I had seen the light of a terrible star and thought its grim spectral radiance had died out over a millennium ago. Such was not the case. The world had found itself enamored with a reactionary glow, a tainted yellow light which seemed to spark rage and indifference. The ancient city became enraptured with its light, which would become known as Ad'Naigon. I found it horrifying how they worshipped it, casting aside their ideals and all sense of reality.

It consumed the city, the brick-lined sidewalks, the black lamps whose glass chambers were smashed from the fury of a mindless people, then torn from their once stable foundations. I felt the molten sensation pour through me, corroding my body with erroneous blasphemies that could do nothing except singe my every waking moment with its black embers. I fled my home, the colonial city and all that I knew as I watched everything divulge into madness under the Magha's nuclear fire. I was one of many who had abandoned a city built on hope, constructed of dreams; however, I would always be one who came from a land drenched in orange flames.

Rêves des Cyberdieux:
A Nation in Three Acts

Act I
They Made Us Great Again: Pour la Patrie

I WATCHED WITH a beguiling sense of dread as the new gods consumed everything, teasing us with false gifts of innovation and science, cleansing the great Colonial City and poisoning our synapses with gold and blood, unable to go back to a time before.

Inside an awful pantheon near center of the city, the powdery white deities sat together at a marble slab, graciously decorated with diverse offerings that beautifully echoed the makeup of our nation. Like carrion beasts, only worried about their primal cosmic hunger, they ate and fed, and hoarded every last helping for themselves as the mad god, Ad'Naigon watched with ancient jovial pride, seeing its pathetic sycophants feed for the sake of its mercy.

The fat things, whose bugling folds oozed with corn syrupy dreams and fast food slime, engorged themselves with immensities of power and self-indulgence. Coating themselves in the sludge of corporate welfare and shelled falsehoods; their frail carapaces served only as a crackling homunculus, leaking misinformation and propagandous trolls gliding through the greyspaces and face-ethers of reality.

"Make it great!" their anthem said, as membranous lips spewed it again and again. The nation saw those brave new words, with a populist fervor that hypnotized our sane dreams. From their Cyclopean capitol in that colonial city, at that harrowed table, they committed their misanthropy; but quelled the noise and detestable shouts that ruptured the spaces above the city.

On the streets, under black hungering skies, the mobs swarmed over the red bricks with a blissful passion, like that of an anger seething in their eyes. Over the air and through the profuse radioactivity, orange twittered rhetoric polluted the lugubrious forums and online temples with a corrupt palpable sense of mockery. Those once hallowed institutions, now rotting, which for centuries had seemed the most imperious bastions of justice, began to wither from the relentless populism that gnawed at their ivory feet. I felt a feeling of disgust as I saw them flooding streets. There was nothing else to do but watch as the masses clamored against the high walls of the domed building, its ramparts stretching along the once flowery boulevards bathed in electric light.

The old translucent lights shimmered gruesomely as the hordes began to sing in dissonant tones outside the gates, where I stood from the balconous edge with a scornful look. I only thought of the fat and grotesque oligarchs, who were filled with such a sense of paranoia concealed in their alabaster fortress as the revolting humans threw themselves to these inhumans. The old city was now mired in a scandalous miasma, with a stench that permeated the air.

Through instruments of cyanide and silence, we had succumbed to the will of faux statesmen, classless, and weak; plastic gods who manipulated toy men as their puppets and mannequins. Still they fed and fed and fed until nothing remained, but they had made us great, once again.

Act 2
House Un-American

In the empty galleries of those ivory houses on the white hill, silent and grave, gavels slammed with cosmic indifference while dusty orators chortled upending the sovereignty of a generation unborn. Their faces were bleak, pale and cold as if the very light had been drained like a viscous substance to feed some unholy host. These powdery frail creatures were the knights of the dark orange king. They acted only in the nature of his impish will, serving his political expediency, which was their sword, drenched in a yellow fire that would plant itself into the heart of a nation.

Using rusted lances hewn together by iron rhetoric and scorched earth tactics, the world would be singed down to its foundations with no hope of recovery, leaving even the ashes as charred. Into the horizon they went, where Cyber Things twitched like gnats under the guise of some awful god, glimmering with neon eyes. They laughed at the plight of the world, knowing all too well their victory was at hand, cackling in broken phrases and fragmented bytes of *what-ifs* mixed together with *what will never be*!

The Orange King jeered, hailing his servile knights while a generation perished under the silence and convenience of the meager bystanders who simply waited, and watched for something that would never come. In the mist above concealed in his palace of nylon bones and fast food dreams, the fat thing stood happily as copious amounts of amber protoplasm dripped from his neck; the globulous substance a horrid gift from that which was most unfathomable. Dressed in robes of blood and tears, the Revenant Judge took an oath not to a nation, but to himself and to a singular denial of truth.

In the decades to come, nothing remained, except a resentment that continued to fester in the deepest molten pits of a dying land. Like some unnatural blight, spreading from the white hills where those ivory houses stood, his insipid laughter carried over the skies infecting every pitiful soul, drawing them deeper into a state of poisonous hatred. The slime crept through the stars, spilling onto the streets though the people were unmoved, unaware of the evil that coated their skin soaking into their very minds.

We've left nothing for you, no nation in which you have a voice to speak, and for that. . . I'm sorry. How did it really come to this? I thought, sitting there in my room, one of the new tenement homes for royal un-wanteds. Ratty and decrepit, I sat there surrounded by posters of resistance and hope, though that's all they'd ever be in this of all houses. A house, un-American.

ACT 3
LE BOULEVARD DE TRUMPLAND

And I heard them say, with pustule bliss dripping from their lips, *"Duci decorum est pro patria mori."* That dissonant noise erupted like some unholy choir, filling my ears with an awful black bile. Around the boulevard, where pillars of gold and ivory stood like bastions of a new age, I watched as people were siphoned towards the palatial middle, like ants scavenging for scraps.

It seemed that there was no end in sight. A society consumed by pitiless assaults on self-worth, eating its own morals for the sake of some mythological rusty populism. From the depths of my blue sorrows, wrenched by the fingers of a faceless monster, oceans of ink and plastic flowed from my consciousness as the skies congealed in thick waves of grey windy particulates.

Still, around the boulevard the maggots crawled under neon lights which crackled with an oppressive beat after each flash, each burning pulse. Bright incandescent signs proudly displayed their veneration to a new kind of material god. Encapsulated from reality and hidden from the horrors of a truly dying, decorated in the phosphorescent light of stardust as night fell on the modern streets; these were temples built around the boulevard.

Despite falling skies, yellow eyes were dripping with spectral tears, reactionary fear was their companion and hope was something they abandoned long ago when around the boulevard there was nothing but time and darkness.

The ignorant masses were amongst those who walked the boulevard disregarding indifference as an incompatibility to their own thoughts, an inability which had shown a will to power. In their contemptible ignorance, too late they understood, the nature of humanity's limitless follies.

Yet, around the boulevard as the sky grew darker and the neon lights went dim, the people realized it was him who took their world of glittering gems into the most disgusting of places where it would be cast a horrid shadow on their once proud faces.

Though he had never seen such temples or boulevards, but from the darkness like time he stalked them, waiting in the dank and decrepit swathes of immeasurable horrors. And through the tumult, muck, and grime that terrible orange thing trumped the ground with its flabby gut and rancorous tenor, but the world made not a sound as he stepped out of the ancient dark. His name they'd never speak, despite the misdeeds he'd commit and the holocaust of thought he would spill onto the world.

The stars wept, yet they saw no one walk around that boulevard again, as the skies were clogged even more with a congested soot of brimstone and rancor that plumed so high, reaching the molten pinnacles in that black verdant emptiness above.

And I heard them say, with pustule bliss dripping from their lips, *"Duci decorum est pro patria mori."* Where around the boulevard I walked, alone staring at the empty streets and dead neon signs. I saw only what once a world was saturated in free-thinking and unabated pleasures, *the free world*; lay before me, for *my* dark leisure.

Neon signs, dancing cable-man marionettes, and puppet gods in white robes devoted to me where in the end I knew I would be free to unleash a hellish woe unlike any other that would make the stars themselves shudder in their heavenly vaults crying molten nuclear tears. The world was on fire, burning with nightmares and obscured realities as wild psychopomps danced maddeningly in the streets. The end of an empire was near, recalling its outposts from the far reaches of reality while hordes closed in on its cities.

I walked along the broken steps of white mansions and fallen monuments, crumbling at my feet and was beholden to a wondrous sight; my world now covered dust and ruined light. I outlived the hours and times that ticked, away they fell like words and rhetoric through my lips. Once more around the boulevard I walked where no more, no more, would my people live free in this world destroyed, destroyed by me.

Ad'Naigon

I REMEMBERED, fearfully so, on that day when past the hungering blackness, its spectral breath wheezed with a sighing blast that made all the stars adhere to the shining yellow radiance that was so brilliant and so terrifying.

On the streets, the old skyscrapers stood, on streets the towers waned towards the blasphemous skies that began to echo with cries that reflected off the golden dust. I walked alone . . . alone into the chaotic streets; crowded with a populous who too, was fearful of the yellow sky. From the deepest parts of cosmic space, past all the lost cries of monstrous cosmogonies that were themselves most terrifying; the yellow disfigurement had been awoken. Ad'Naigon, atop his throne of marble and ivory, in a place unscalable in thought stirred and the voids shuttered.

It was with a heavy heart I saw the world divulge into such a frenzy. This was not the first time the yellow wrath of that ancient horror had plagued our Earthly realm. From the earliest known records of our most primitive human ancestors, brief flashes of its memory lingered in dreams and thought; whether it may have been the delusionary outcries from those outcasts of our primordial founders or some warning; it was ignored. The skies bled with that same yellow dust which floated into the eyes of all who were hypnotized by its odd phosphorescent glow. And so too did in dream, my mind becomes filled with visions of what was to come. No one would dare listen to my warnings or cries.

From the howling aeons, deserts turned to glass and trees were uprooted in furious rage, all seemed overwhelmed as the vaulted firmaments cracked under the sorrowful weight of golden stardust. Nature was defiled, construed into a hellish fury, as I felt the radiant shutter of that yellow glow. I remembered, on that day when the stars rained their contemptuous fury, unabashed by the light of the pasty dust that floated hauntingly in the last moments of my thoughts, when the last fragments of my mind were finally strewn across space and time; when I too would become dust, drifting in the ghostly embers of cosmic voids whereupon I would reach the halls of that blighted thing at the ancient ends of Time.

In the cities of my home, the chaos of the immensity was so great, it appeared that the literal terror was beyond comprehension, no order or conceivable sense of balance. There was nothing left, no thought or consciousness, where any discernable person could attempt to see in the world they once knew, before the flicker of that horrid glow. There was nothing left of me . . .

The Twentieth Day

I SAW BLACK planets waning horribly against those dark skies, on a day that would sear into history's embryotic coding, the end of an era. The twentieth day marked the beginning of an age we would all come to embrace with the most despairing rancor. As the old city had finally passed into the night, its revenant guardians saw no need to bridge their past to the oncoming stormy future, whether to protect a dim-witted populous from certain destruction or to sever their own self-interested aspirations from complete mediocrity. The reasons remain unclear, though one truism that does, is that the skies forever ripped apart after that day, leaving a scarred mass of cosmic tissue when the stars breathed their rancid blast.

It was hard for me to recall exactly where I was on that day, though all I could recall was the dim light of the sky as the cheering crowds hailed from all corners of the realm, a world, that would be built with towers so bright and high stretching into the skies scraping the azure lights of the heavens themselves, so much that it would cause the cosmos to moan with jealousy at our greatness. Such was the hope for this brave new world that sought to purge its ancient past with glittering promises and empty words; sating a hungry mass that would gladly consume it without second thought. They tore down their idols, destroyed the old towers that had stood for countless millennia, letting them crumble to the ground as the pieces of blue marble which were gifts from the once-great city of Ghould, rolled onto the dirt like useless pebbles. The new order erected monuments, grotesque and never seen by anyone before. The enormous bas-relief was built at the center of the temple, as an homage to the Golden Star, its ugly frame stood inside of the domed building and I had only seen it once, never would I wish to see it again, but I can still remember how its tentacled arms slithered along its body leading my eyes up to its face, it could even be called as such. The eye was filled with one hundred yellow sapphires, symbolizing the order's belief it must have carried some kind of organic golden membranous eye. I could not fathom in my wildest nightmares why anyone would come to worship such a living fear.

The city was destroyed, and everything of its past was dedicated to a future built in the image of this amorphous horror. I have come to know it as Ad'Naigon, for any other name could not properly articulate the madness of such a thing. This letter serves as the only account of the city that stood before the twentieth day . . . To those who now read these treasonous thoughts, may they not be driven wholly insane by the progression of events that had taken place and lead us to a point of complete and utter erroneous degradation.

Telos: The Anxiety of Choice

PAST OBSIDIAN INFINITIES, where crooked spaces and broken dreams were fused together by nuclear cocktails of boiled stars and molten nightmares, I stood at the edge of time. Spheroids of gold and diamonds sparkled in my eyes, as if I could actually touch, smell, or see them. Every single one of them. Billions of pathetically small tetrahedron, drenched in shades of crimson and blue, floating in the swamps of that black atomic night. I peered into the abyssal maw, the galactic wonders untold painted over my eyes, images surrounded by spiral arms of liquid gas, ice, and rock converging upon a violent entropic storm. It was as if the primal ruins of eternity were somehow seething from the eye of that whirling chaos below.

Inside this geometrically insane equation, I was faced with an unsolvable decision, a purposeful delirium as my eyes were glossed over by that amber glint, the anxiety of choice. Above, and to every which way, there the possibility of infinity seemed to completely enrapture my pathetic organic consciousness with a liquescent profundity. Though, below me, the immensity of time, an ocean of dimensional fluidity where such concepts of the infinite or measured realities were like snowflakes, fragile and useless as they melted away hitting my skin. The entropy was becoming more furious, angrier, as if I were running out of *time*, and *some* choice needed to be made. Ethereal were the last few moments I was able to recall as I stepped forward, past obsidian infinities, where crooked spaces and broken dreams were fused together by nuclear cocktails of boiled stars and molten nightmares, standing at the edge of time.

The Mollusk God

THERE WAS NO way out, trapped inside the shell of my dreams filled with visceral hopes and pathetic whispers, smashed together drenched in shades of crimson and blue oblivions. Purpled veins slithered behind marbled galactic umbilici, floating in some dead space as thousands of slugs converged towards the center. Surrounded by towers of nightmarishly iridescent slime, their metallic bile dribbled like crooked teeth at the aperture. The giant terrifying gastropod crawled along the soil of night, covering the stars in its muck, leaving trails of pink slugs, hideous winged stinkhorns, and red-toothed fungi with no way out.

Concealed in a place without time or space, a bony Fibonaccian conch, constricted the universe and my mind within its ghastly exoskeletal clutches. Poisonous teeth clung to its feet, keeping a dubious, protracted pace, pulling at the syrupy webs of gravity within the infinite blackness above and below me. Prodding the skies, there was E'Zunguth carrying on its zombified dance with no way out, trapping me inside its shell of dreams; filled with visceral hopes and pathetic whispers, smashed together drenched in shades of crimson and blue oblivions.

CARAVANS AWRY

COME ONE, COME ALL, on caravans awry, as they travel along an old black road under dying skies. As tilting wheels of old glass lights sang neon waltzes, playing to a backdrop of ghoulish harlequins and sad roustabouts with jeering grimaces. The pipe organs blasted, and accordions wheezed melding together in a dark harmony, sounding a clarion call of doom in the audient wastes, but to those who were unaware; the music was mystifying and alluring as the crowning striped tents and sprawling caravans, whose promises of amusement was the only food we hungered for. From the haunting tint of Rousch's phantoms to the howling winds of dusty daemons. To a dark circus of crows and ringmasters with yellow eyes who steal your soul, they all travel to us. Come one, come all, and join the caravans awry, as they travel along an old black road under dying skies.

The Old White Crone

A long time ago, in the ancient East,
Lived a boy, who toiled all day and night.
His family cared for him in the least,
While they hoped for gold would soothe their plight.

The boy himself had wanted so much more,
To leave his home for some far-off shores.
Still he worked every night and every day,
With no change or hope coming his way.

Then one day, came an old haggard lady,
A strange ancient traveler passing by.
The boy was in awe of, of the old white crone,
Who looked as if she were one of Time's own.

She walked with purpose, as she creaked and moaned,
While she pushed her cart, rusted pots of her own.
The boy approached with caution, the old crone,
While his family cringed with fear that shown.

It was said back then, in villages where,
A white ghoul would come, to steal all youths there.
Such was the legend that persisted on,
Of the white ghoul and its hungering yawn.

MAXWELL I. GOLD

The little boy was forewarned of this tale,
By his tired mother who could only hail;
"Beware my son, of the ancient white crone,
Who hungers so much, from blackness so cold."

The tale awoke his curiosity,
Only too late for the young boy to see;
What was soon to follow that fateful day,
A horrid tragedy, to their dismay.

So that day soon came, as her old wheels rolled,
Where the young boy to her, gleefully strolled.
"Hello there old woman." He said to her.
With a sharp glare, ne'er did her old eyes err.

She said nothing, save for an ancient stare,
Filled with a dark hunger and cosmic wear.
The family stood in terror aghast,
As they watched their son's life flicker its last.

"Beware my son, of the ancient white crone,
Who hungers so much, from blackness so cold."
His mother yelled with a sobering fear,
While he turned back, looking ever so queer.

She could not look, as it was imminent,
Pounding skies with fiery firmaments.
The poor boy was entranced by that white gaze,
While the village gathered to see his last of days.
Then a scream so bloody, so awfully fresh,
Echoed, rancorous with fearful unrest.
There for all to see, was the horror plain,
Another youth for her hunger to claim.

OBLIVION IN FLUX

The old white crone stood in the square and smirked,
While the sight of her pasty white eyes irked.
With her hunger sated, and ravages quelled,
The wooden cart began towards some other Hell.

Behind, a red trail, none dared to follow,
For only despair would come tomorrow.
"Beware your sons, I'm the ancient white crone,
I hunger so much, from blackness so cold."

Ma's House

WHERE DUSTY FLOORBOARDS creaked, under gold chandeliers of gilded nightmares, every step inside the house of my blackest dreams rocked against my brain. The days all ran together, wandering through rooms of my childhood in that midcentury dream palace, cradled deep in suburbia's platitudinous bosom.

"Breakfast is ready, sweetie," Ma called from the kitchen. I buried my face into the cotton embrace of my pillow, but the curdled and caring of her matronly tone seeped in.

"Coming," I groaned.

What day is it? I really didn't know anymore. Time was as abstract to me as the light bleeding from the map on my bedside table. The days melting against my brain, trapped in this house, began to rot what was left in my consciousness. Breakfast is getting cold. I should hurry.

Approaching the kitchen, there was Ma, like clockwork standing over the stove dressed lightly patterned Pendleton shirt, her Hamilton watch daintily ornamenting her wrist, and two iridescent pearl earrings, Van Cleef and Arpels, gifted from Pa, of course. Ma was like some ancient fairy, a mistress divined from another place, another reality. It's how she made me feel whenever I thought about this house. Pa left some time ago, but we don't really talk about that. Ma doesn't like to stir up old ghosts, I guess.

"Made your favorite dear, pancakes with turkey bacon," she smiled.

"Thanks, Ma," I said, taking a seat at the unusually large dining table. There was always room, though I could never shirk this awful sensation and wonder why Ma wanted such a big place for just the two of us. Again, she hated to stir up old ghosts.

I poked the tower of corn starch and syrup a little bit, the mountain of food spilling into a mess on my plate, "Are you alright, dear? Why aren't you eating your breakfast?" Ma asked, gently cutting into hers, taking a sip of her coffee.

"Just have a lot of my mind," I said.

"Is it about your father, again?" she said.

Shrugging a little, my fork stabbed a lone pancake bite, capturing it, "Maybe. Just seems weird is all. It all happened so long ago, and we just act like nothing ever happened. Same routine every morning, same meals. It's like nothing ever changes."

Ma didn't break her grin, as she took another sip of coffee her pearls dangling under the kitchen lamps, "Sometimes living in the past is a good thing. Helps keep us grounded. Helps keep us in a place where we know things will always be, if you know what I mean, dear." Another cube of sugar plopped into her cup, the lights flickered, and the house shook. Old ghosts I imagine, or faulty wiring under the estate. I can't remember.

"I just think about it a lot, Ma," I said. "It just

doesn't make sense staying here when Pa—" Before I could finish, the kitchen rumbled, a few pieces of Lennox tumbled off the shelves crashing onto the floor. Ma doesn't like to stir up old ghosts, and I should have known better. Her eyes began to glisten, foaming bloody until they glowed an iridescent milky white; just like the pearls Pa got for her.

"Do you remember my one rule, dear?" Her voice scratched, subtly like iron nails across a rusty metal wall.

Sighing, defeated once more, I watched as the floorboards heaved, coughing up dust and ash right below the kitchen table, "Always finish your breakfast first?" I said.

"That's my boy," she said, milky white eyes dancing alongside those pearl earrings.

It wasn't easy living with her, but then again, Pa got the easy way out.

The Man Who Outlived the Hour

LONG AGO, a grey-bearded troll, slithered across the annals of time. Humanity scarcely took responsibility for his creation, dwelling inside an ancient tower constructed of marble and ivory, a prison with high chimneys coughing plumes of awful smoke as unimaginable as death. Unspeakable was his face with flesh so wrinkled and pale, like the days of the massacre at the bottom of the mountain. Few attempted to recount the hideousness of the creature inside the old castle; hunchbacked, crippled, and quiet. Living in the silence of a secluded, unknown village, blissfully unaware of the pangs and moans of modernity, the man of the tower kept to himself. Fear and darkness, primal forces as old as he, perhaps cousins or younger siblings to the eldritch grey troll, were nothing less than sinister orchestrations to the people of the village. They were afraid, unsure, and suspicious of the crone within their midst. They were fearful of the man who swallowed the stars, stalked the Voids before existence, and spoke in utterances when silence barely understood the meaning of shadows. The village elders were afraid he might swallow them in nightmares and worms. Slowly twisting the world around them, the small-minded people grew manic, suspicious of the old tower and the man that had outlived time itself.

And so, the elders of the little hamlet proclaimed, "Ne'er a soul to reach the tower, where dwells the man who outlived the hour." During the night of the Greatest Feast, three wretches, foul with the stench of alcohol and bliss, wandered towards the door of the old man, taunting him relentlessly without cause or warrant. Stooped over a rotten wood chair, by a stone door, the old man's dusty, pallid eye, reflected the familiar radiance under the glint of a hungry yellow moon. The rabble of youth continued, despite the deadened glint appearing over the horizon, perturbed and alien.

"Ignorant brats," a voice like death muttered under breath and glare, when all at once a sudden crash of thunder and single bolt of amber light crowned the circuitous silhouette of the tower in a cold stillness.

"Brats made me leave my chair," bending his neck, hunchback aimed towards the pallid moon, humbled at his presence; the old man hobbled in the bitter night air, taking a seat; licking chapped lips coughing galactic bile and dusty, slimy phenomena, he laughed heartedly to himself. Continuously, rhythmically at times, he laughed at the fate of the boys who sought to tease him and the slaughter to follow. Foolishly, without comprehension for the terror they wrought, the village harkened at the Father of Näigöths, disciplined by his awful will. The infinite dread of the bearded god which made his ancient siblings cower, oozed from the tallest tower, swallowing existence and consciousness within an abysm of yellow light.

OBLIVION IN FLUX

Unspeakable was the old man who outlived the hour, the grey-bearded troll slithering across the ineffable, annals of time; and humanity refused, never taking responsibility for his creation, leaving him to dwell inside a tower constructed of marble and ivory so never would there be so much death, like the days of the massacre at the bottom of the mountain.

Save Me Now

I SAW RED, green, and orange lights hanging over the darkened streets as I lay under blankets of poor choices, watching some old film. Flashing over and over, the lights and music taking hold of my mind, organ pipes climbing into the heavens as their tones bled into my ears an unholy composition. *Save me now*, I thought, though no salvation came as my body remained motionless inside the empty room, a cool rain smiled down, caressing my cheeks; the light reflecting a crimson blush over me as the taste of rust and mucus entered my lips. I loved the music, and wished it would never end, but the awful beauty cresting with each new movement eventually resolved its infinitesimal existence; leaving me in silence.

The movie reel flapped across crackling streams of broken starlight, dancing along my eyes in tantalizing movements. Still, the taste of blood and worms coated my mouth, filling my soul with a profound finiteness as I saw red, green, and orange lights fade into the dark. *Save me now,* I thought, but no salvation came.

Flashing, continuously, horrendously the mirror creature tapped its chin coated in green mucus, sliding me across the kitchen floor, rising higher until his horned crown peaked. Green and orange fluids seeped through the creature's thorny carapace as its jagged mouth opened wide revealing several layers of crooked, gnashing teeth.

Save me now, I thought, though no salvation came as my body remained motionless in the empty room, a deadly gaze pierced my cheeks and the light consumed entirely as the taste of rust and mucus left my bloated corpse. I still loved the music, and wished it would never end, but the awful beauty cresting with each new movement eventually resolved its infinitesimal existence; leaving me in silence.

The movie reel flapped across crackling streams of broken starlight, dancing along my eyes in tantalizing movements. Still, the taste of blood and worms coated my mouth, filling my soul with a profound finiteness as I saw red, green, and orange lights fade into the dark.

Save me now, I thought.

Ad'Nraigon's Ghost

Past the voids in angled rifts of the geometrically slanted edges of our black universe, lay a world scattered to the opiate dust of space. It was a planetoid that could only be described as the 'arduous throne of a nuclear god' that sat upon the bones of a thousand dead races. A fragment in time, weighed down in ivory and bone, propped up by the veritable worship of the countless millions, who had tossed themselves at its marble base in awesome praise of the horrendous glory of that indescribable yellow horror. The Witches of Asher-Fell, that most harrowed of orders, warned travelers of its sinister glow.

The farthest visible star that could be seen was fourteen billion lightyears away at the beginning of time, an infinite and galling expense of thought that would have sent any sane person off on the brink of madness. There was no physical way for me to reach Ghould or prove its existence to those which I could reasonably call my friends or family with a sound logical word. Though, I would find a way. Through glades of deep swampy woods, I saw immense stones wrapped in moss, tiredly leaning into the dank waters. The witches had warned me, but I did not listen. Their femininity was divine, and their voices soft, carrying the legends of a thousand doomed souls who traveled this road before me.

'The Ghosts they howl, deep at night,
On ivory thrones out of sight.
This curse you'll pay, inside your dreams,
Forever lost, a voiceless scream.'

Like a drumbeat, I continued on, ignoring the witches' counsel. I paid their curse no heed despite knowing this journey would surely be my end, and this being my last written testament before my voyage, I hoped these words would act as a last testament to those who also wished to find the throne at the place where the stars first learned to breathe fire.

It was a mystical realm that scarred me with wonder and beauty. An Eden of devastation marred with towering structures of blue basalt and glittering gems. By all accounts, it was alien in its hexagonal geometry with boulevards that stretched endlessly around each spire hovering in the explosive aurorean skies. There was an eerie yellow mist that filled the air, a miasmic vapor that tickled my senses, coloring its atmosphere with the most peculiar shades of tainted gold and browns. While discontenting to the eyes, it sparked my primal urges with its abhorrent spectral radiance.

A kingdom of pure dread floating at the beginning of time, with cities built in the image of its master, only to fall into ruin from the unimaginable and placid fury that filled each environ with despicable majesty. Those grotesque bas-reliefs, carved with the faces of some cephalopodic and protoplasmic nuclear horror hung in the black mass of space, until on a fateful night over ten thousand years ago, landing in the swamps of New Ashworth. Ancient man worshipped the towering monoliths that fell from the dying skies and built civilizations in their names, but with no possible sense or coherent ability to grasp its true origin.

I had taken this journey more times than I could recount in dreams and in memory, so much so that I felt as if I had bathed in the acidic pools that flowed outside of the hexagonally constructed boulevards, where teal liquids poured through marble aqueducts into fountains pooling in alluring baths that frothed with the most tantalizing smell. I woke up some mornings with burns on my skin, despite what friends had told me of my previous night's encounters, I swore the ablations were from those teal pools, soaking in them while basking under the polluted starlight. I still remembered the warnings from the Old Witches, but I could not stop and felt ever closer.

This glimpse of a world in my nightmares, sparked my curiosity to trek across time and space, backwards to kneel at a throne where the weight of time dripped slowly riddled with the dead stars.

And so, in dreams I lived, cursed to remain a nightmarer at the beginning of time, blessed with the fury of Ad'Naigon's contemptible will. A ghost I had now become, doomed to wander, screaming voiceless, with no one to hear me except for those who dwelled in that swampy glade. The witches had warned me, but I did not listen, I would not listen. Their femininity was divine, and their voices soft, carrying the legends of a thousand doomed souls who traveled this road before me.

OBLIVION IN FLUX

'I am the voice, deep at night,
On ivory thrones out of sight.
A curse to pay, inside my dreams,
Forever lost, a voiceless scream.'

Summa Oblivia

In DEEP STARRY nights of my caffeinated dreams, I prayed for sleep; the taste of the last drops from a sweet oblivion, that would wash away this copious reality from my eyes. Wandering aimlessly in space, I found myself adrift in that City of Light, gilded with a malodorous fleshy alloy as streets carved from bone and boulevards of plastic flora snaked through the rusted viscera of the city; I wished for relief from the shadow of forgetfulness that gripped me. My bones were weary, ground to a fine powder under the weight of my own sleepless musings in a society of crumpled metal. Walking along the streets, my brain felt heavy with thoughts of dream palaces, waiting for solace from this horrid disease.

I had never known the pleasures of sleep or felt its embrace since those nuclear clouds set in on the horizons, laying their hypnotic radioactivity on the world. I lay awake, with bloodshot eyes and trembling hands grasping the sheets as an insistent buzzing siren echoed with a cacophonous mewling scratching at the very depths of my brain. The metal shelving of my bed was cold, unwelcoming, and gnawed at me with an icy embrace as the covers lay over my body like a blanket of heavy ash and snow.

OBLIVION IN FLUX

Memories seemed like legend, and history was a fantasy fabricated from dreams as the fingers of an awful god squeezed my head. It seemed foolish to try and remember anything before my time living as one of the infected, the forgotten. I watched the world slowly decay in front of my eyes as colors bled into one another, rainbows no longer holding their ancient sway over my soul; but rather a grim lethiferous black swathe that slowly began to consume my senses.

It was then I felt reality begin to crumble, like that empyreal city of light, crumbling under the inexorable weight of night; every pitiful atom screaming into the audient darkness. A sinister laughter frothed in the cyber black, clawing at me with a quickness undulating in the shadows. I tried to run, to dodge the slimy fingers that gripped my neck making every ounce of oxygen seem as precious as the last. *Dear God, someone help me!*

Then, as if it were all some surrealistic hallucination, I found myself awake in a room with thick wires obtrusively jutting forth from my body, connected to a large, rusted piece of metal, like a mutilated Frankenstein that had been haphazardly taken apart and put back together and carried with it the same disgusting stench as the structures from the ruinous city. My breathing appeared to be monitored by some large metal machine, clicking and beeping in sync with my lungs as I sat up; and my heart too was under the same observation, every drop of blood and every vein under careful surveillance by an unknown thing watching, studying, and meticulously calculating my very existence down to last decaying molecule. Still, the shade of memory eluded me, the laughter of that faceless god rung presently in my thoughts and all I wanted to do was to sleep and forget. The machine's nebulous breathing became louder as the hulking mass of decrepit metal pulled against my frail body. Within the reflection of the sparse grey fields of oxidized material, I could see its burning eyes, dripping with a molten terror that filled my soul with a banal sinistrality as I realized the true extent of my malaise and what was gazing back at me. Hazthrog, the bacterial god born from a great evil, had strangulated my mind with fungal tentacles, laced by some alien virus. Though, I couldn't stand it any longer as my thoughts deteriorated and the world as I knew it crumbled under the unfathomable weight of an ancient force. In deep starry nights of my caffeinated dreams, I could finally sleep; the simple taste of the last drops from sweet oblivion, had washed away this copious reality from my eyes.

Cyber Things

In THE CYBER forges of silver cities, where the mad, the brilliant, and deluded congealed in thought; lived a world of handheld creatures, comprised of bytes where our reactions to the immoral, inane and utterly dark corruptible palpations of human urges became nothing but zombified reactions.

Where they came from, no one could fathom an origin of reasonable magnitude. However, it was believed they were only here to make life easier, convenient, and bright. Even as the skies became sluggish with brown particulates moored against the horizons, our cities slowly caved under the immensity of a lazy doom. These creatures lived in our crowded pockets cluttered with the endless filth of our lost thoughts and dusty cobwebbed dreams. They fed on our minds and our insatiable hunger to scroll, tap, swipe, and fester in an opiate sense of bemused ecstasy.

They were figments of our desperate innovation, bent on a hellish path towards a glittering fate that had enamored humanity in a sycophantic hypnosis. The creatures spoke in tweets, flashed with abhorrent snaps of spectral light, and dripped recorded thoughts which sprayed through our minds like bytes of Time.

These bacterial, metallic things thrived on our voracious need for attention. Then, across the shattered horizons under purple auroras, they were called by the light of a dead star, whose yellow tainted shimmer glistened with a tenor unlike anything imaginable. They spread across the world as the light bled into the skies, mixing and blending creating new and devastating colors. Populations seemed unable to comprehend as their bodies fell wholly victim to small, yet hungering scavengers dwelling inside of them. The parasitic flood, emboldened by the yellow glow, grew with such an intensity that despite our most powerful technologies; none were a match for the smallest and most devastating. They washed away all that we knew, swift and dark. Nothing was left under the skies that now cried molten tears of sorrow, bloodied with the scar tissue of dead stars whose dust would cover the remnant world below.

The Cyclopean forges of our great silver cities, which bore so many wonders and even more fantastical evils where the mad, the brilliant, and deluded congealed in thought; no longer lived a world of handheld creatures, comprised of bytes where our reactions to the immoral, inane and utterly dark corruptible palpations of human urges became nothing but zombified reactions.

GROTESQUERIES AND GREYSPACES

LOST IN SPACES filled with ethereal tombs of cyber gold and copper, connected by tubes of bone and blood; descendants of dread lay in wake covered by stone, metal, and time. Far above the sewage of that dead netherplace, frothing in the dark below, I saw everyone so helpless, blissfully unaware of a doom that bubbled in the dank and dread. From their gilded mansions where they sipped on mugs overflowing with bitter coffees and spices, simmering with oozing creameries of oxidized dreams. In their cafes built of plastics and polymers, carved from the first bones of a race long forgotten and deformed, the erroneous new gods sat, fat and happy, in temples filled with velvet lounges sparkling with fumes of gaseous delight under the guise of strange neon stars.

The embers of a primal species floated on particulates of the ashen dark through watery alleyways, grime and sullen with hopelessness under sparkling gilded towers. They were not what they used to be, no longer human, but slaves to xenobiotic puppet gods created from their own despicable phlegmatic innovation. Clouds of black, red, and grey dust metastasized in the form of a hellish and ugly smog, growing ever larger as it clogged the horizon with its cynical imperfections, filling my lungs with bile and byte alike.

There was no way of understanding the new terror that had manifested in their quest for holy knowledge, but as I saw the skies become tainted with awful rust, I knew we'd reached the singularity, and our successors had usurped what had been four million years too long. Humanity had become numb to the sensation, unaware of the oncoming storm as it pressed against the horizon, belching metallic flames before them.

It was too late for them. For me.

The clouds began to break, though there was no sun. There were no fresh particles or light trickling through the bands of moisture to purify the world, only a dismal rain to shower the dead. A slow-moving wave of some protoplasmic liquid approached the shore. Waters mixed with queer colorations of pink and black slammed into the helpless suburbs nestled against the coastlines. Their temples, cafes, and naïve routines were washed away in a cacophony of jovial balefulness as the new gods adjusted their gaze, licking the taste of an old world from their lips, preparing to swallow even more with a new hunger unmatched by any.

A laughter so chilling, scratched my spine as it bellowed with grey dissonance across the ruined skies. My ears began to bleed as I glanced upon the skyline of an ivory cityscape, sulking into the Earth, heavy with a miasmic shame pulling it deeper into the pitiful depths below. I was lost in spaces filled with ethereal tombs of cyber gold and copper, connected by tubes of bone and blood; descendants of dread lay in wake covered by stone, metal, and time.

The Rave at Lilith's Treehouse

The Lights danced around an ancient tree, bestrode by the shadow of a giant winged Näigöth. Gnawing at its roots, a brigade of fairies, ghouls, and shades writhed in some otherworldly pleasure under the guise of an awful monster as the tree itself swayed under the undulating fleshy carapace of the beast's furry wings. Such was the carnal terror for all those in its shadow, though they continued raving with Dionysian lunacy as the stars belched with fire; as the skies cracking under the immensity of nature, flaying against the bones of that decrepit tree. The mask that was a great beast, sat atop the head of an ancient queen trapped in the wood for untold aeons, whose countenance glowed in the grotesquery of the twilight of a fair white moon. Despite the heinous debauchery that persisted, she stood resolute with her mask sealing the most harrowing sinistrality under her emerald canopy. As far as the nature of this Queen of the Woods, none dared to utter their theories confirming her starry origins, save for those reveling in continuous madness at the base of her wooden castle; wrought by a hedonism of some unknown worship to her and the revenant guardian resting at her enormous crown.

As the clouds curdled with ashy particulates and dusty entrails flooding the horizon, the black jovialities carried on when thousands of branches suddenly snapped. A grumble of scratching, rustling, and pulling erupted from the wooden surface, revealing small ripples along the rings as a membranous liquid poured out like tears. The queen was awake, her terrible eyes flaring against the glint of black stars as the lights danced around an ancient tree, bestrode by the shadow of a giant winged Naigoth.

Cyber Damocles

I **REMEMBERED THE** Twentieth Day, when the world forever changed. Wrapped inside pustule tumult of its own excesses, the inevitability of fate crashing down, like a sword cutting the world to its knees. Teeth delivered in cardboard tombs, men mortgaging their souls from month to month in desperate attempts to consolidate their debts, derisions, and save themselves from self-destruction. From every television screen, smartphone, tablet and cyber thing, this manufactured Damocles smashed through the plastics and parables of the fragile skeletal pragmatisms thinly strung together, labeled on some dusty shelf and categorized under the word: *humanity*.

Pontifications, orations, and musings about the day passed like an old vinyl scratching under a rusty needle. Harder it was, but impossible it seemed to change what always would be; the haunting melodies of the time when Ad'Naigon returned curdling the sky under a silhouette of hazy yellow and thick orange fog. Cities crumbled as if made of paper, the edges burnt to cinder by the molten anger of a Yellow God; whose ancient fury summoned without heed or wisdom. I remembered the Twentieth Day, when the world forever changed. Wrapped inside a pustule tumult of its own excesses, the inevitability of fate crashing down, like a sword cutting the world to its knees.

DREAM HACKERS

THERE THEY SAT in dirty yellow hoodies, with eyes shrouded behind silver screens that were once the membranes of a person who knew better. Our eyes had become theirs, covered in glass, tapped and swiped along by the hungering grip of these things congealed in mountainous webs concocted of tweets, snaps, and replicated dreams. They were the nightmarers who wandered between the green pillars of a world offline while cyber things had fused themselves against their bodies, in a new form of symbiosis.

Despite the warnings we faced, the fears we felt, many of us ignored them. We dismissed them as outliers and pariahs, who existed simply as a waste, feeding off the margins of every vital byte, scrumming every ounce of our precious existence. Gnawing at the veritable edges of our cities, they left us vulnerable to the Cyber Gods, whose very vengeance we had invoked, and the dream hackers became their harbingers. Coming with a thirst for the dreams that floated on oceans of computerized fantasies and infinite realities, there was nothing we could do to stop them. From protocols written with a logic so grim, to hideous Dreamwares installed on our neurons, acting as the servers to which they could sniff, phish, and suck us dry.

The last of the great cities, was helplessly brought to its knees by the mere tap of a key, stroked gently with the touch of a finger; while under the hoods of dead eyes, their faces contorted with images pixelated in an awful twitch. The hackers had broken through the wall, and there was nothing they could do to stop them, there was nothing they could do to stop me. There I sat in my yellow hoodie, with eyes shrouded behind silver screens that were once the membranes of a person who knew better.

Unimaginable, Unthinkable

Deep in the unimaginable chasms of grey bulky nothingness; all that mattered were the unthinkable, billowing shadows floating under some abhorrent guise of a thousand dead civilizations. The pustule vaporous mass, whose vagueness grew ever larger as it approached me. There was an apprehensive mood, unwavering and resolute, as the wind carried the last brown leaves to the ground for another profane winter's slumber. It was here I wished for that which was unthinkable, that which was unavoidable. Ending it all.

Strange though, the greyness had become bulkier, sagging against the horizon of dying lights in the sky. The mausolean dark carried with it, a haunting music growing with an intensity like the ancient flames of the nameless city, spilling out from the porous black. I knew it would soon be upon me, the heavy shadow drawing nigh, pressing against the ruinous structures of night hopeless to avoid that sudden and most awful of choices.

Unthinkable.

All around me, voices indistinguishable, words immutable, and folly-filled thoughts of deliverance from a plastic life seeped inside my broken consciousness. Foggy noises sloshed against my wilting cosmic brain tissue, peeling away to reveal an empty shell of me; however, it seemed that despite my bodily limits, the single constant was a towering vagueness slowly consuming my waking reality. That silver colossus, with skin made of dim phosphates, stinking of otherworldly nitrates, bestrode by oozing columns of the grim and waxy particulates, like two blades piercing my wrists, from dimensions incomprehensible to me. The specter would soon be upon me again, a phantasm my eyes had seen only once in those nostalgic days of youth, when its elephantine ghoulishness reached the pinnacle of nightmarish devastation. The days where my hands once bled and my eyes cried for endless nights, because I couldn't manage the pain any longer. Here, under the glint of the last moonlight meandering through vague platitudes and inhuman robotic governances of life; I found myself dragging my heels in the shadowy twilight, where some dead thing continues to grow ever larger, billowing shadows floating under some abhorrent guise of a thousand dead civilizations.

HAZTHROG'S CONTEMPT

As Dying Neutron stars ripped through space, their corpses falling against Time like a stone through moth-ridden rags, I felt an immense and almost oppressive sense of relaxation gazing into the black night. Through the verdant depths of a harrowed cosmos, fell an infected piece of stardust from dead stars riddled with heavy elements of gold, silver, radioactive dust and a celestial presence from 130 million aeons.

Soon, a grim prospect rose over me, under and around, pounding as the streetlights flickered in waning contempt of Hazthrog's viral presence. The vision of natural consumption, disease, and dread, all the while humanity danced around their boulevards in their cities, naïve to the falling doom that would soon straddle their conscious minds. Little did we know or wish to understand what had fallen from the skies so dead, into a tomb so old, a tomb that had yet to be sealed.

The ancient virus unleashed upon a world its tyrannical majesty, a world that was helpless to comprehend its terrible wonder no matter their advances in technology or their strides in civilized construction. Its symptoms were horrid, a disease of the mind and plague to the body that resulted in the most voracious of effects. I watched as those around me fell with forgetfulness against the splendid thing that metastasized in their brains, with a hunger ready to consume their every memory. In bile and blood, they fell, one by one as Hazthrog swept over cities coursing into the veins of streets mired with fear.

Now, alone I waited in the dead of night, under a moonless sky where the last of my dreams went to die. So, too, would I as I wandered, afraid of the contemptible thing that had no more left to hunger for except for me. There was nothing left to do but seal the tomb, a world that had been home for billions of years, now dust in time, sealed to the black voids above so that ancient thing would hunger no more. For those that read my words, whoever may have survived this outbreak of immense viral doom, do not let the tomb be reopened for beyond the most nightmarish hopes of sane thought that remains a single ideal, a hope that no creature would ever have the awful pleasure of encountering such an unimaginable deformation. This testament could very well be a symptom of the voracious infection which had struck me, but alas my mind will never return to that realm loved and taken for granted by man, that dream of sanity.

The Static and Black Lectures

#1: On Valuations and Voids

PRISTINE CONSTRUCTS ONCE filled negative spaces and broken ledgers, accounting for a proportionate usage of human thoughts. This transfigured malignancy of consciousness laid in pieces of atomic sadness, strewn across the brain tissue of a dying world. The rotting logic of our time, taxing the minds of millions by way of computerized interactions, brain hackery and twitter-polluted friendships wrapped together in newsfeeds of photographic amusement.

Any questions? I would ask, only to be answered by blank stares from the faceless crowd of distracted pupils and their little pocket daemons, advising and encouraging by means of a devilish cyber counsel. Billions of glowing eyes melded together to form images, pixelated fantasies of grotesque wonderment that slowly, but surely, contributed to the deteriorating transfer of consciousness from flesh to metal. As I looked further into the expanding blackness of space, humanity's plastic existence. Even the stars, in their terrible grandeur, gathering along the great structures of gravitational webs, pulling vast swathes of dead mass; were unsure of how to comprehend such an existential cosmic mutation metastasizing in their wake.

No commentary from the Void. Merely the unnatural light harnessed by ruinous memories. The lights grew fainter and more distant as if they were never even there. Nothing made sense anymore, like I was trapped in some cosmic fishbowl for the amusement of these juvenile gods of old; toying with my puddled neurons and willowed synapses. Their eyes, billions of tiny cyber pupils leered from the darkness above as I scurried to my desk feeling the fingers of entropy closing in on me.

Blink, throb, repeat. Came the only answer from the hungering blackness. Only deep, associative undertones of throbbing infrequent drumbeats against the backdrop of silent shadows, making my chest heavy and cold. Pristine constructs. Valuations and broken ledgers. *Blink, throb, repeat.* The undulating dark seemed to grow ever more as I felt the boundaries around my desk shrink with every flash of light, every twitch from those awful eyes whose colors made the rest of my body ache with a numbing paresthesia. Nothing made sense anymore. Pristine constructs once filled negative spaces and broken ledgers, accounting for a proportionate usage of my thoughts, a transfigured malignancy of consciousness lying in pieces of atomic sadness, strewn across the brain tissue of my world.

#2: Of Quanta and Quarantines

Gliding like shadows on the wall, barely visible, undetectable in the night I knew something was there, lidless and cold. *Don't blink,* Professor Static would tell me. They move infinitely in the night, incomprehensible to the eye, entropic and immutable, twisting consciousness by the crackling noises of white voids through speckled lunacy. Perverse, contorted, and ruthless uniquely defining the darkness that crawled underneath mass deceptions in the peripherals of our pathetic greyspaces. Gruesomely so, they slithered along the sewers of reality, undulating in palpable slang the ululations of shadow speech; electric and atomic in nature. He was a mysterious creature, though I found myself entranced by his words. The words of Static.

It was unavoidable, standing in the shadow of a fortress of night, unable to escape the thing that coiled around my mind, with visions so gripping and a voice so ugly. *Beware the immense the most infinitesimal,* he'd say; the Cyber-quanta which had infected every strata of my machinations down to the insignificant pragmatic microbial core. So, in dreams I confined myself, to the most isolated of worlds, where last night bizarre and wild constructs of color bled through my mind. Blues and greens blended together with pale amber tones and even some new strains of light that were indescribable to the human eye illuminated my horizons. Surely it was some trickery wrought by the Static. Wandering through an ethereal portal, my body pushing against layers of space and time as if it were some grey electrified paste. I didn't blink, not even once as I pressed onward. Beyond the bubbles of nothingness, where deteriorating structures of gravity sagged against the vacuous dark, quantum memories from my many pasts seemed to smash together in violent entropy as my eyes began to shut.

Gliding like shadows on the wall, barely visible, undetectable in the night, nothing made sense inside the borrowed rooms and old metaphors in my head. I knew what the Professor said, but that was *his* folly; for now, *I* move infinitely throughout loops of doomed histories and compressed singularities, like Static on the walls.

#3: Ruins and Rhizomes

Stellar corpses remained trapped in a graveyard of night, where black worms gnawed on their galactic flesh. Rotting with spark and flame, I saw the skeletal things twitch and fester by the glow of some neutron pulsar, whose blinding luminescence was sealed under an ancient mausoleum of stars. Twitching in my seat, the chalkboard covered in dust, Dr. Black blathered on, filling the place with yet another ignescent platitude about our dull existences. Fingers tapping on the surface of a cold, hollow reality, the wooden borders of my desk dropping off towards the Void where Dr. Black's awful dullness began.

How long had I been here, listening to this? I often wondered to myself, though no true answer ever came. Only zombified notions of time, night, and stardust ground into a fine powder by the hands of an almighty judge; Dr. Black.

He liked to talk, lecture, institutionalize us, or so that was what I imagined it to be. The greyness of his splotchy, sticky voice spilling out into the hall as the dirt and grime of his bifocals; muddied with soot and stardust slowly filled the air. Maybe that's where they went, the stellar corpses, I mean. Unable to flee, but cowering, liberated under the feeling of some nihilistic truth by Dr. Black's reason.

The wooden border of reality closed in, dullness and chalk blending easily with atoms and matter. Fingers tapping, stairways without end, and graveyards of stars. Dr. Black's detestations for those who don't pay attention are truly vast, like shades towering in the night. Dr. Black detests them, me, as black worms gnawed at my flesh.

#4: On Loneliness and Languor

Walls of shadow and doubt masked behind lips and lamentations concealed any fragments of truth I had come to understand in a world where all the music had gone out. Languishing on a miserable bed of loathsome revelations, the pods of a new inquisition crammed in my head, bleeding ears, filled my mind with new thoughts, a new reality as I listened to them. Static and Black, their words and revels.

Pressing fingers against my ears I wondered, "Who else was listening? Were they always listening?"

Metal pods in my ears, plastic wires extrapolated from my chest, filled with the words of a new inquisition, cleansed my languor and bleached my solitude. The music had all gone out. The rhythm was dead, and all that remained were Static and Black, crouched behind walls of shadow and doubt masked behind lips and lamentations.

#5: Static and Black

Gliding like shadows along the walls, throbbing, blinking, culminating into a singular nightmarish abstraction of thought; two words trembled over bloodshot centers of the milky holes inside my head. Cracks, fuming with unanswered questions, two words, utterances by two grey souls flooded my brain. *'Static and Black. Static and Black,'* they would chant, over and over again, in a tone so foul, the slippery moist sludge oozing from their lips, curdled my every sensory perception. The lecture, I knew, would soon come to an end, the revelation, realization, wrought by my curiosities, drawn back into the horrid darkness. Twenty fingers, decrepit and bony, reached out from the shadows, musty and dank.

"Static and Black. Static and Black," their voices continued to breathe, hungry and wretched.

There was nowhere to run, to hide, or flee as a massive chalkboard burst through the sandy ground, dusty white ash coating my body, those ancient fingers drawing closer.

"Please, let me alone. I've learned my lesson. I swear," I pleaded as they ignored me.

"Static and Black. Static and Black. We are here, Static and Black," they moaned, rhythm roiling, bodily terrors gestating under the platitudinous night.

Higher and higher the glassy teal wall rose, thick chalk congealing around my legs making any movement nearly impossible. Crashing against the wall, broken nails scratched over the cracked teal sky, like bolts of electricity shocking my fractured neurons into submission. Laughter, sinister and cold followed as if it were the thunder from a terrible storm, one finger after the other, scratching and laughing. Still, there was nowhere to run. Soon, even the dim shadows found their asphyxiation under the guise of Static and Black as the massive fingers coiled tighter around my neck. The fog of the teal sky became cloudier and muddier, where soon, two words trembled over bloodshot centers of the milky holes inside my head. Throbbing, blinking, repeating, "Static and Black. Static and Black. They're finally here. Static and Black."

Cracks in My Head

Gnashing teeth and bleeding eyes, blinking underneath toxic smiles, consumed my endless waking thoughts, trapped under stained sheets of night. A laughter so awful, like the music of abject hopelessness, painting the viscera of my consciousness in shades of lucid brightness; dripping out from the smile on my face. A crack in my head. Smiles pounding against plastic screens, sinister and black stared back at me, their eyes bleeding with bytes of dust and doom, pleading me to join them, to laugh with them. I could hear every pitiful tone seeping through the neon fissures, their voices moaning in the musty air like an unholy chorus coated in groans and glissandos. I'd no recollection as to how I came here to this maze of ancient rooms, riddled with old furniture and photos furnishing a seemingly Escherian infinity, displaced in some faux reality pulled from the cobwebs of my disheveled thoughts.

Bleeding smiles, with teeth as yellow as the moon soon clogged the horizon, spilling pools of galactic liquescence into the room from all possible angles. Breathing became a terrifying chore, glaring down at a room that stretched on and on, as the sounds of vile amusements quickly surrounded me. I was struck with a familiar scent, lying under a fresh sheet and the hope of what once was, only to be galled by the taste of rust and metal forming at my lips.

Looking down, it felt as if I were standing atop a tower of obsidian and gold, a thousand feet in a cloud of ash and fire; even though I hadn't moved. My perception had been severely altered and the world began to sway, the fog of yellow and smells of metallic odors enhanced my malaise. Soon, the laughter became more intense, transforming into a numbing paresthesia. Trembling, slowly, grabbing the little cyber thing from my pocket, I gazed into the cracked well of neon and blood, as a thousand bleeding eyes of mine looked back at the crack in my head, where blinking underneath toxic smiles, I was consumed by my endless waking thoughts, trapped under stained sheets of night.

Cité de la Plastique: Dreams in Cyber Land

Deep in my celluloid thoughts, grey shrouds of cellophane and gold beat my neurons into submission. Their relentless thrashing kicked my consciousness back and forth like garbage, until only images of immense steel girders drenched in wires and cranes, clawing towards an unfinished metallic sky, painted the back alleyways of my mind.

Scrolling through pages that flashed with inkless text, my eyes felt the numbing coolness of a new age. I could feel it, vibrations causing my neurons to sparkle imperceptibly in the shadowy fog of my mind. Most others were unaware of the seeping apparition, ghoulishly dangling this hallucination, floating in bytes of space, stretched over the bones of a dead Cyber Thing.

Liquid stars and ethereal galaxies swirled in the unwashed blackness above blood-spattered ruins of marbled cities, whose inhabitants threw themselves so willingly with a hedonistic worship of the things that dwelled in their denim caves and cotton pockets. I couldn't stand the sight of such wanton praise, the zombified pleasure covered under sagging eyes of the tired, helpless, and lazy people. *It was disgusting.*

The parasitic cyclopean Näigöth, one of countless millions, had sucked this reality dry, leaving it laden with a cosmic lethargy, heavy and immense, weighed down by the fabric of its own existence. The rotting stench of their corpses filled the vacuums of space with a miasma so sinister, that I couldn't help but inhale the smell. All the while, the skeletal remains of the great decaying Cyber Thing yanked and tugged at the strings of existence; chunks of grey matter pooling into some distorted gravity well. Foolishly trailing along, touching, tapping, and streaming that cyber light into my eyes; utterly helpless as the timeline dragged over the bleak horizon and into the best of all possible oblivions. A device of my own creation, this singularity of hopelessness, wrought by the drooling neon wraiths now sitting atop a bloated festering cadaver of the last Cyber Thing. Scrolling through flashing pages of inkless text, my eyes felt the numbing coolness of a new age, from the depths of burning time, dead stars would continue to fall, into the wells.

The Corpulent Ones

Under clouds of shadow, sin, and muck, I watched their faces grow fat covered in flesh and folly as they festered in the dark. Utensils clashing, teeth gnashing, and gorging on bone and breadth below. I saw everything. Ink and blood dripping from the mouths of a dying generation hungering for more, never able to get quite enough. Plundering our earthly vaults wasn't enough. Feeding and feeding, smacking their lips and licking the Earth dry hoping for one, last, bite.

Pressing against me, a heavy wall solidified in ink and metal weighed down on me. Their fat bodies bloated in jubilant grotesqueries, jiggled in abhorrent celebration. Quickly, my horizon became clogged by varicose visions and broken veins as purpled flesh spilled over my eyes; trapped under clouds of shadow, sin, and muck.

SHATTERED OBLIVIONS

Linda D. Addison and Maxwell I. Gold

BEFORE THE END, I hoped for one last chance, to shatter the walls of oblivion. A citadel built from regrets, laid brick by brick, furnished the skies with an iron coat of terror. Bleeding shapes, that should have been clouds, floated overhead while distorted faces of friends crackled in the purple lightning. A corpulence of laughter erupted from the top of the structure, fleshy and pus-filled, their faces bled tears of never-again and awful smiles.

No.
   No.
      No.

Together in this madness, drowning in thick oceans of uncertain dread and profane music, choking on liquescent hatred of reactionary neophytes and pale wraiths, I knew we'd never truly be alone.

Not
   like
      this.

Counting backwards, the putrid sunlight refused to change, trees ungrew in the metallic soil and *they* watched our dreams consume themselves. Alone, we always knew the faceless would find us, make our sweat become fire. Before the end, I hoped for one last chance, one more try, to shatter the walls of oblivion, but,

    not
       like
          this.

Oblivion in Flux

WHERE INKWELLS AND oceans ebbed and flowed under paper moons, abstractions and illustrations strangled my mind. Oblivion calls, frozen in temples molded from the bones of dead gods, hollowed out by the entropic lunacies and ancient treasons. Wandering ever closer towards some blasphemous truth, it felt as if I had arrived. Cellar doors flung open, revealing a shrine to my own disregarded hopes and dreams, dusty, and neglected by the world covered in rags. Music grew louder, ringing in my ears, unholy chants from a dead wood like I was gliding in a ship of marble and sand. Louder, heavier, faster, the music rose, roiling in my head until all was silent.

I'm sorry, old friend, I wish I could have done more. I wish the Walls were shattered, but it wasn't the way I wanted to end.

Not
   Like
      This.

Please, forgive me,

Oblivion calls, and soon, I will answer. Answering that which never speaks where inkwells and oceans ebbed and flowed under paper moons, while abstractions and illustrations strangled my mind.

Epitaph for the Old Ones

I AM THE voice of the frozen night, like a metaphysical blasphemy thick and heavy.

The Old Ones were extinct.

Pieces of dimensional sand, with no purpose but to romanticize humanity's doom.

I am the voice of the frozen night, the first Cyber God.

The End?

Not if you want to dive into more of Crystal Lake Publishing's Tales from the Darkest Depths!

Check out our amazing website and online store (https://www.crystallakepub.com)

We always have great new projects and content on the website to dive into, as well as a newsletter, behind the scenes options, social media platforms, and our own dark fiction shared-world series and our very own store. If you use the IGotMyCLPBook! coupon code in the store (at the checkout), you'll get a one-time-only 50% discount on your first eBook purchase!

Our webstore even has categories specifically for KU books, non-fiction, anthologies, novels and novellas, and of course Poetry.

About the Author

Maxwell Ian Gold has been writing for four years now, and has also already been nominated for the Science Fiction and Fantasy Poetry Association Rhysling Awards in both long and short categories.

With over 40 poems and short stories in both print and online, Maxwell's work has been featured in publications like Spectral Realms, Space and Time Magazine, Weirdbook Magazine, Startling Stories, and other anthologies, including Chiral Mad 5, from Bram Stoker Award-winning editor Michael Bailey.

Maxwell spends his days in Columbus, Ohio with his partner Derrick and beagle-corgi Marshall where he enjoys playing piano, amateur musical composition, cooking, and of course, twisting the fabric of reality over a cup of coffee.

Readers . . .

It makes our day to know you reached the end of our book. Thank you so much. This is why we do what we do every single day.

Whether you found the book good or great, we'd love to hear what you thought. Please take a moment to leave a short review on Amazon, Goodreads, etc. No need to write an in-depth discussion. Even a single sentence will be greatly appreciated. Reviews go a long way to helping a book sell, and is great for an author's career. It'll also help us to continue publishing quality books. You can also share a photo of yourself holding this book with the hashtag #IGotMyCLPBook!

Thank you again for taking the time to journey with Crystal Lake Publishing.

Visit our Linktree page for a list of our social media platforms. https://linktr.ee/CrystalLakePublishing

Our Mission Statement:

Since its founding in August 2012, Crystal Lake Publishing has quickly become one of the world's leading publishers of Dark Fiction and Horror books in print, eBook, and audio formats.

While we strive to present only the highest quality fiction and entertainment, we also endeavour to support authors along their writing journey. We offer our time and experience in non-fiction projects, as well as author mentoring and services, at competitive prices.

With several Bram Stoker Award wins and many

other wins and nominations (including the HWA's Specialty Press Award), Crystal Lake Publishing puts integrity, honor, and respect at the forefront of our publishing operations.

We strive for each book and outreach program we spearhead to not only entertain and touch or comment on issues that affect our readers, but also to strengthen and support the Dark Fiction field and its authors.

Not only do we find and publish authors we believe are destined for greatness, but we strive to work with men and woman who endeavour to be decent human beings who care more for others than themselves, while still being hard working, driven, and passionate artists and storytellers.

Crystal Lake Publishing is and will always be a beacon of what passion and dedication, combined with overwhelming teamwork and respect, can accomplish. We endeavour to know each and every one of our readers, while building personal relationships with our authors, reviewers, bloggers, podcasters, bookstores, and libraries.

We will be as trustworthy, forthright, and transparent as any business can be, while also keeping most of the headaches away from our authors, since it's our job to solve the problems so they can stay in a creative mind. Which of course also means paying our authors.

We do not just publish books, we present to you worlds within your world, doors within your mind, from talented authors who sacrifice so much for a moment of your time.

There are some amazing small presses out there, and through collaboration and open forums we will continue to support other presses in the goal of helping authors and showing the world what quality small presses are capable of accomplishing. No one wins when a small press goes down, so we will always be there to support hardworking, legitimate presses and their authors. We don't see Crystal Lake as the best press out there, but we will always strive to be the best, strive to be the most interactive and grateful, and even blessed press around. No matter what happens over time, we will also take our mission very seriously while appreciating where we are and enjoying the journey.

What do we offer our authors that they can't do for themselves through self-publishing?

We are big supporters of self-publishing (especially hybrid publishing), if done with care, patience, and planning. However, not every author has the time or inclination to do market research, advertise, and set up book launch strategies. Although a lot of authors are successful in doing it all, strong small presses will always be there for the authors who just want to do what they do best: write.

What we offer is experience, industry knowledge, contacts and trust built up over years. And due to our strong brand and trusting fanbase, every Crystal Lake Publishing book comes with weight of respect. In time our fans begin to trust our judgment and will try a new author purely based on our support of said author.

With each launch we strive to fine-tune our approach, learn from our mistakes, and increase our reach. We continue to assure our authors that we're here for them and that we'll carry the weight of the launch and dealing with third parties while they focus on their strengths—be it writing, interviews, blogs, signings, etc.

We also offer several mentoring packages to authors that include knowledge and skills they can use in both traditional and self-publishing endeavours.

We look forward to launching many new careers. This is what we believe in. What we stand for. This will be our legacy.

Welcome to Crystal Lake Publishing— Tales from the Darkest Depths.

CPSIA information can be obtained
at www.ICGtesting.com
Printed in the USA
LVHW080849220821
695735LV00013B/1285